TENSE MOMENTS

Creed glared at the swell's hand, noting a gold and rhinestone ring. He shifted his view to the fellow's face: blue eyes, a wisp of brown mustache, pale complexion, and a sneer of arrogance. Creed judged the fellow to be close to reaching his majority, although not quite there yet. He wrenched his arm free.

"The girl said '*No comprendo*,' friend. Or don't you understand Mex?"

With iron in his eyes and ice in his voice, Creed said, "*Yo entiendes español muy bueno, muchacho. ¿Y tu? ¿Cuánto sabes tu, cabrón?*"

The swell's upper lip quivered in anger. Men close to them ceased their conversations . . .

"What are you, mister?" the swell finally managed to stutter. "Some sort of wise ass?"

Creed's Choctaw ancestry came to the fore as he allowed his features to go stony, while his left hand unbuttoned his coat. "You may apologize for that remark, sir," he said. . . .

Berkley Books by Bryce Harte

The CREED series

CREED

COLORADO PREY

BRYCE HARTE

BERKLEY BOOKS, NEW YORK

COLORADO PREY

A Berkley Book / published by arrangement with
the author

PRINTING HISTORY
Berkley edition / November 1992

ISBN: 0-425-13507-1

A BERKLEY BOOK ® TM 757, 375
Berkley Books are published by The Berkley Publishing Group,
200 Madison Avenue, New York, New York 10016.
The name "BERKLEY" and the "B" logo
are trademarks belonging to Berkley Publishing Corporation.

PRINTED IN THE UNITED STATES OF AMERICA

10 9 8 7 6 5 4 3 2 1

To my sister
Tommie
with love

REAL HISTORY

With the exception of Pedro's Cantina in Nevadaville, every business mentioned in this work was a real going concern in August 1866. Every person with the exceptions of Creed, his family, and various villains lived in the places mentioned at the time of the story. Every geographical feature mentioned is accurately named for the time of the story.

Of particular interest is Sheriff William Z. Cozens, a legendary Colorado lawman. As detailed in this story, Cozens faced down more than his share of lynch mobs. The story of how Gilpin County got its first jail is the same story told over and over by Cozens himself.

Addie LaMont was Denver's first madam, and the story of how she came to be a prostitute is true.

All details concerning the Colorado Gold Rush of 1859 are also accurately detailed.

For a good read on the early history of Central City and its environs, the author recommends *Gulch of Gold* by Carolyn Bancroft.

1

A buck! thought Creed. Big fellow, too. Just look at the size of those horns.

A gurgling mountain freshet split the three score yards that separated Creed from the deer. A breeze stirred the leaves of the quaking aspens around them.

Creed sat perfectly still atop his gray Appaloosa, downwind of the stag, hoping that the animal wouldn't see or smell him or his horse, that it would continue rubbing its antlers on the trunk of the mountain cedar.

Unwittingly, the buck granted Creed his wish by minding its own business. Rutting season was coming, and it was time to remove the itchy velvet.

Hunger pangs stirred within Creed. His heart beat rapidly with the primitive excitement of the hunt. His mouth watered at the thought of eating a venison steak.

That's an awful lot of meat for one man, he thought. But it'll keep a long time up here in these mountains. It's plenty cold enough at night, and if I hang it in the shade in the day time, it'll be all right for quite a spell.

Creed bit the tip of the middle finger of his right glove and pulled his hand from the garment. He allowed it to dangle from his mouth as he reached slowly for the Henry rifle protruding from the scabbard on his saddle. He took the gun by the stock and slowly pulled it free. As quietly as he could, he worked the lever to cock the hammer and inject a cartridge into the magazine. He lifted the rifle to his shoulder and aimed carefully at the buck, sighting on the animal's rib cage just behind the front shoulder. He sucked in a deep breath, let it out slowly, and squeezed the trigger.

BANG!

Creed worked the lever again, ejecting the spent shell and loading another in case it was necessary to shoot the beast twice.

The buck lurched, startled by the explosion from the rifle's barrel. It took a few steps away from the cedar before it dropped dead.

Sure that his quarry would stay put, Creed eased the Henry's hammer into the safety position and rested the rifle between the saddle horn and his groin, while he donned the glove again. He picked up the Henry, set the butt on his right leg with the muzzle pointed skyward, and urged Nimbus toward the fallen deer. Hunter and horse wove through the rocks, trees, and brush to the stream, crossed to the other side, and continued wending their way to the buck, covering the distance in a few minutes. Creed halted the Appaloosa beside the dead animal, replaced his rifle, alit, and tied the reins to the cedar that the buck had been scraping. Eyeing the game, he recalled that he hadn't shot a deer since before the war. Good lord! he thought, how long ago was that? It seemed like aeons to him, considering all that had happened since then, but it was only six years back. He shook his head with both sadness and surprise, heaved a sigh, and set about dressing out the carcass.

Creed removed his gloves and stuffed them inside their respective pockets of the long, gray duster that he wore when it was cold or the weather was inclement. He removed the outer garment and draped it over his saddle. He pulled off his brown cloth coat and placed it atop the overcoat. He unbuttoned the sleeves of his flannel shirt, then rolled them up to his elbows. He pushed the sleeves of his cotton undershirt midway up his forearms. Last but most important, he drew the Bowie knife from its sheath on the saddle.

Flat ground was rare in the mountains. This locale was no exception. The slant was fairly severe, pretty close to forty-five degrees in this spot, which suited Creed just fine. It would make gutting the buck easier for him. He placed the carcass on its back so that it lay with the head uphill. The next step was to kneel down, grab the deer's windpipe, and cut through it with the Bowie. A wisp of steam escaped from the wound. Now the messy part. Creed slit the hide of the animal's underside from sternum to anus, being careful not to cut into the peritoneum membrane surrounding the guts.

From the cover of a copse of small pines several yards behind Creed, a pair of dark eyes watched closely as the hunter continued to dress out the buck.

Creed had come to the mountains seeking solitude. He wanted to be alone for a while, away from people, until he could sort out a few of the problems facing him. He needed time to find himself again, to make peace with himself, to regain his self-respect and the confidence that he wasn't an evil person because he had killed several men in his short lifetime of twenty-four years. His plan would have him ride until the last man that he saw was two days behind him.

Sometimes even the best plans don't work.

The dark eyes continued to spy on the hunter kneeling over the dead deer. The right moment to move forward with great stealth would be soon in coming.

Having made all the necessary cuts, Creed jammed the Bowie into the dirt beside him. He dug his hands into the buck's hot, bloody chest cavity, took hold of the windpipe above the heart with both hands, and pulled with all his strength. When the organs broke loose, he rocked backward but didn't tumble as his buttocks came to rest on the heels of his boots. A steamy vapor rose from the carcass and vanished into the cool mountain air. Creed continued to remove the animal's innards.

Seeing that the hunter was engrossed with the work of gutting the deer, the dark-eyed man stepped quietly from the copse of pines. His soft-soled rawhide boots made no noise as he stalked closer to Creed who continued to remove the entrails from the dead buck. Now only an arm's length behind Creed, the watcher stood poised to attack, but he had no weapons except his bare hands—and Creed's Bowie.

Out of the corner of his eye, Creed noticed a shadow on the ground come beside his own. He pulled the last of the organs from the carcass and tossed them aside as if he suspected nothing out of the ordinary. He allowed himself to glance at the silhouette for an instant before feigning a return to the task in front of him. Damn! he thought. It's a man! A second look. Oh, damn! thought Creed. He's an Indian.

He was an Indian, a Ute warrior attired in plain buckskin tunic and trousers. His rich black hair was parted on the right side, but it was also braided in two tails with leather thongs. He was stout and powerful of build with a strong jaw and stern expression.

Creed reached for his knife.

The Ute attacked, throwing himself full force atop Creed, slamming the hunter to the ground next to the deer carcass. Having pre-empted Creed's attempt at the Bowie, the Indian's right hand grabbed the handle of the knife and pulled it from the dirt.

Creed wanted to retaliate, had to fight back. He rolled to his right, hoping to throw the Indian off him and give himself the opportunity to draw his Colt's from his waistband. If unsuccessful at this, then at the very least he hoped to stop the Ute from stabbing him with the Bowie in the next instant.

The warrior anticipated Creed's maneuver and allowed the Texan to turn over beneath him. As soon as the Texan was on his back, the Ute dropped down hard on his gut, driving the wind from Creed's lungs and leaving his victim powerless against further attack. The assailant held the knife high over his head, but he didn't bring it down into Creed's defenseless body, the deathblow forestalled because he felt the grip of Creed's revolver digging into his right buttock.

I'm a dead man, thought Creed.

Not yet, he wasn't.

The Indian bounced to his feet in one instant, and in the next, he reached down with his left hand and drew Creed's gun from the Texan's pants. Coming erect, he cocked the weapon and aimed it at Creed's forehead.

Regaining some of his breath, Creed ignored the Colt's in the Indian's hand and focused on the Ute's eyes, glazing his own orbs with calm complacence. "Never let your enemy see inside your heart," he heard his Grandfather Hawk McConnell saying.

Recognizing a man who wasn't afraid to die, the warrior didn't shoot. Instead, he tossed the Bowie aside, shifted the Colt's to his right hand, bent over, grabbed Creed's shirt front with his left, and jerked the Texan into a sitting position. Straightening up again, the Ute planted the sole of his right foot on Creed's shoulder and pushed him down the slope.

After tumbling several yards, Creed managed to stop himself. He hurt. He hurt bad. In the gut and in his head because it had struck a rock along the way. He sat up slowly, painfully, and looked back up the hill at the Indian kneeling over the pile of entrails. What's he doing? wondered Creed. He forced himself to stand and took a tentative step uphill. His legs hurt, too.

The warrior stood up. He heard Creed making noise behind him and turned to see what this hunter would do now.

Creed stopped moving toward the Indian as soon as he saw that the Ute held the deer's liver in his left hand and was eating it voraciously. The Texan shook his head. "Why didn't you just say that you were hungry?" he said as if he expected the Indian to understand him. "I'd have shared the deer with you."

Although he seemed to understand Creed, the Ute made no reply. He simply continued eating the liver, his face dripping dark red blood from the organ.

A second of scanning the Indian told Creed that the revolver was on the ground and the knife was in the Ute's right hand again. He took a cautious step forward.

The Indian waved the Bowie at him as if to tell him not to come near.

Creed stopped to study the situation. Maybe all he wants is the deer, he wondered. He took another step, this one slightly to the left.

The warrior shifted with Creed's movement, maintaining a stance between the Texan and the deer. He also continued eating the liver.

Creed moved up the hill while veering to the left.

The Indian maintained a defensive posture between Creed and the buck.

That's it, thought Creed. He wants the deer. He can have it, but I'd still like to have my gun back.

Creed circled back to the right until he was close to Nimbus. He permitted his view to shift to the Colt's in front of the Ute.

The Indian stopped eating the liver, put a foot on the six-gun, and said, "No."

Creed backed away. "I have a rifle on my horse," he said. "I can get it and kill you."

"No, I think you will not kill Ouray," said the Indian confidently.

"No?" queried Creed, surprised by the Indian's command of the language. "Why not?"

"Ouray did not kill you first."

Smart fellow, thought Creed. He speaks English, and he knows that I'm sick of killing. "Ouray? Is that your name?" When Ouray made no reply, Creed introduced himself, "I am Slate Creed from Lavaca County, Texas." He added the last as a matter of habit, not because he thought it would make any difference to the Indian.

Ouray's eyes widened a bit as he said, *"¿Esta' Tejano?"*

Surprised by this response, Creed blurted, *"Sí, Tejano."* As soon as he said it, he began regretting it. Comanches, Apaches, and Kiowas hated Texans and vice versa. Maybe this fellow hated them, too.

Ouray smiled and said, *"Muy bueno, mi amigo. Tejanos estan mi amigos."* He stepped back and kicked the revolver toward Creed. *"Su pistola, mi amigo."*

Before moving to pick up the Colt's, Creed raised his hands in front of him, showing the empty palms to Ouray, as he said, "Look here, *amigo,* my Spanish isn't perfect, but I understood what you said. Texans are your friends, but I'm just wondering if I can trust you not to stick me with my own knife if I try picking up my gun."

The Indian looked offended. He straightened up as tall as he could and said, "Ouray has honor." He threw the knife down at Creed's feet. *"Tejano* has honor?"

Creed bent down, picked up the Bowie, wiped it clean on his pants, turned around, and replaced it in its sheath on the saddle. Turning back to Ouray, he said, "I can't speak for all *Tejanos,* but this one has honor."

Ouray smiled, nodded, and said, *"Muy bueno, mi amigo."* He held the raw deer liver out to Creed. "Eat?"

"I prefer to eat liver after it's been cooked," said Creed. "*Gracias* anyway, *amigo*."

"Eat," insisted Ouray.

"What do you say to me starting a fire and cooking us some of that venison instead?"

"Eat!"

"Well, I guess you did spare my life. I suppose it's the least I can do to show my appreciation for that." Creed accepted the chunk of liver that Ouray offered to him, and he bit into it, although with great reluctance. Blood squirted from the corner of his mouth and dribbled down his unshaven chin as he chewed the delicacy. The taste was warm and salty but little more than that. At best, the liver was edible.

"Muy bueno, mi amigo."

That's what you think, thought Creed, but he continued to eat the liver as a show of friendship and good manners. After all, he was the stranger here. Or was he?

2

The last person Creed expected to meet when he rode up into the Rockies was a Ute warrior. He'd been told in Denver and the mining camps and towns that he'd passed through along the way that the Utes had moved away to the west and south and that they no longer posed a major threat. Leastways, not in this part of the territory.

"Occasionally," one old-timer in the region said, "they show themselves in these parts to beg for whiskey or food, but they don't stay long. And once every so often, a fellow goes out prospecting and never comes back. Of course, that ain't to say that the Indians done him in or anything like that. Hell, there's all sorts of ways of dying in these here Rocky Mountains besides getting your hair lifted by some damn redskin. A fall and blow to the head could do it. Griz or a mountain cat could get you. Rattlesnake, too. Get wet and don't dry out right away, and you're sure to get the pneumonia and die. Yep. There's all sorts of ways of dying in these here Rocky Mountains."

In spite of the warning against going high into the mountains alone, Creed continued to look for the solitude that he sought. Until he shot a deer and met up with Ouray, he'd been successful for the two days that he'd wanted to put between himself and civilization.

Creed finished eating the small piece of raw deer liver that

Ouray insisted that he share with him, then he walked to the stream to wash the blood from his chin and hands. Clean again, he returned to the site of the kill to find that Ouray had taken the coil of rope from his saddle, had tied one end of it around the buck's antlers, had thrown the other end over a branch of a tall pine, and had hung the carcass to drain the remaining blood from it.

"You camp here tonight," said Ouray with a smile as he pointed to a somewhat level spot in a small clearing closer to the stream. Then he rubbed his belly and added, "We eat good tonight."

Creed bent over, picked up his Colt's, put the empty chamber under the hammer, then stuck the gun inside the waistband of his trousers. "Nice of you to invite yourself to supper."

"Ouray will make fire now." Ouray began gathering wood and piling it in the little clearing.

"Well, I hadn't exactly planned on staying here tonight, but I suppose this place is as good as any." He unsaddled Nimbus, then helped Ouray with the fire, using a flint and steel to light the dry leaves and pine needles that ignited the kindling.

Ouray hurried to the stream, gathered several rocks of a fair size, brought them back to the campsite, and placed them around the burning sticks. He repeated this process twice more until he had completely encircled the fire with stones.

Meanwhile, Creed took his frying pan and other cooking utensils from his saddle bags and placed them near the fire. He cut three thick slices from the shrinking slab of bacon that he'd brought with him from Golden and put them in the pan to cook down to grease.

Ouray picked up Creed's coffee pot and took it to the creek to fill it.

As the bacon sizzled and filled the air with its delicious odor, Creed skinned one haunch of the deer, cut off several pieces of meat, and put them in the frying pan to cook. When Ouray returned with the coffee pot, the Texan took a little brown sack from his saddlebags and filled it with ground coffee. "This is a little trick that I learned from our cook back in Texas," he said, kneeling beside the fire. "Josephine was her name. She used to take my grandfather's empty tobacco pouches like this one, wash them out to get rid of the tobacco smell and taste, then fill them with ground coffee beans and drop them into the boiling pot of water to make the best coffee you ever tasted. She'd say there wouldn't be any grounds in the cup that way. She was right." The memory brought on a moment of homesickness. "Smart lady, that Josephine," he said softly.

"Josephine? *¿Su madre?*" queried Ouray, squatting on the other side of the campfire with his arms folded over his knees.

Creed shook his head, smiled, and said, "No, she wasn't my mother. She was a house servant. A slave who cooked for the family."

"Slave? *¿Mujer negra?*"

"That's right. A black woman."

Ouray nodded that he understood, but he said nothing.

"I've never met a wild Indian before," said Creed, changing the subject.

"Ouray never met a wild Indian before, too." He shook his head and waved off his words with his right hand. "No, Ouray lies. Ouray met a Comanche one time. Said hello, then Ouray killed him."

Creed chuckled and said, "So you're not a Comanche. That's good. The Comanches killed my father."

Shaking his head, Ouray commented, "Comanches are no good. Comanches kill too much. Comanches kill for . . . for . . . to make them happy."

"Do you mean they kill for pleasure?"

Ouray nodded and said, "Yes, Comanches kill for pleasure. Comanches are no good. Comanches make war on women and children. *Nuche* do not make war on women and children."

"*Nuche?*" queried Creed.

"My people. White men call my people Utes."

"That's what I thought."

The venison began to sizzle audibly in the frying pan, reminding Creed to turn it to cook on the other side.

"Why do you come to mountains, white man?"

"Good question, Ouray," said Creed as he tended to the meat, "but first let's get something straight. I'm not a white man. Well, I'm not all white at least. My people are the Choctaw and Cherokee."

Ouray's eyebrows pinched together with confusion.

"The Choctaw and Cherokee are red men like you," said Creed, "but they come from the East."

"*Tu no eres un indio.*"

"Not completely, no. My other people were whites. Scots from across the ocean. When they came to this country, they married Choctaw and Cherokee women, which makes me part white, part Choctaw, and part Cherokee."

"*¿Qué es ocean?*"

Creed smiled and said, "A great water." He spread his arms to indicate a vast expanse. "A river so wide that it takes many days, even a month . . . a moon sometimes . . . to cross it in a boat."

"A boat?"

Creed recollected a James Fenimore Cooper tale that he'd read once, and the memory gave him the idea to say, "A canoe."

"A canoe?"

Creed laughed and said, "This would be easier if I had a book with some pictures in it. I suppose I could draw something in the dirt, but I don't draw good enough to make you understand what I'm trying to tell you here." A thought struck him. "Where'd you learn to speak Mexican, Ouray?"

"Ouray lived with *los Mejicanos* when Ouray was a boy. Lived in town. Taos. Long way south."

"Taos? New Mexico? Near Santa Fe?"

"*Sí.*"

"Is that where you learned to speak English?"

"*Sí.* White man from mountains teach me. Name was Old Bill Williams. Old Bill was a friend to *Nuche* long time. He turned against my people. We killed him. No good to turn against *Nuche.*"

"I'll keep that in mind," said Creed. He turned the venison again.

"*¿Cómo se llama, mí amigo?*"

"I guess you didn't catch it the first time around. My name is Slate Creed. You can call me Creed if you want. I prefer that because it reminds me of who I am."

"Who you are?"

"It's a long story, Ouray. I'll tell you about it later. After we eat, maybe."

Ouray nodded and asked, "So why do you come to mountains, Creed?"

"Why do you ask that?"

"Many white men come to mountains for gold." Ouray pointed to Creed's saddle and gear. "You do not come for gold. *No tienes un pala o un pico.*"

Creed frowned. "*¿Pala? ¿Pico?*" He shook his head and added, "*No comprendo, amigo.*"

Ouray scooped up a handful of dirt and said, "*Pala.* Dig in ground."

Creed nodded and said, "I see. A shovel."

"*Sí.* Shovel." He made a fist of his right hand and pounded it in his left hand. "*Pico.* Break rock."

"A pick?"

"*Sí.* Pick. No shovel. No pick. You do not hunt gold. So why does Creed come to mountains?"

"Another good question, Ouray. Let's just say that I wanted to be away from people for a while."

Ouray nodded and said, "*Muy bueno.* It is good to be away from people for a while. Ouray do same. Ouray came to this mountain to make medicine. Ouray does not eat from moon to moon. Manitou speaks to Ouray. Ouray sees other side. Ouray learns about time not yet come."

"Wait a minute," said Creed, holding up a hand. "Didn't you just say that you weren't supposed to eat from one moon to the next moon?"

"*Sí.*"

"If you weren't supposed to eat from one moon to the next, why'd you jump me and eat that liver?"

"Ouray is hungry."

"That much I already knew, *amigo,* but why did you give up seeking a vision of the future?"

"Ouray already see other side."

"Is that right?" asked Creed quite seriously, impressed that Ouray had been so blessed. He'd heard about this sort of thing from Grandfather Hawk. Even Choctaw warriors went off by themselves on occasion to seek a vision from the Great Spirit. They wouldn't eat anything for several days as a way of cleansing their souls to receive the message from the spirit world, but once they saw the vision they were allowed to eat again.

Ouray nodded sternly, his stare boring straight into Creed's amber-flecked green eyes.

Recognizing the solemnity of the moment, Creed asked, "Not that it's any business of mine, Ouray, but what's gonna happen in your future?"

"No good, Creed." The Ute brushed off the question with a wave of his right hand. "Ouray asked Creed why he come to mountains. Creed did not tell. Creed tells Ouray first."

"Fair enough. You did ask first, so I suppose I should tell you why I came up here." Not that you'll understand it all, he thought, but what the hell. What else have I got to do for the rest of the day?

3

Denver! The summer of 1866. A great place and time to be alive. Especially if you were a young man of twenty-four years and had survived the most terrible war that your country had ever experienced and your name was Slate Creed.

Since early that year when he first learned that Marshall Quade had moved from Tennessee to Colorado Territory, Creed had planned to go to Denver to find Quade and take him back to Texas where he could be made to tell the truth about the crime that Quade and several others had committed but for which Creed was blamed and subsequently convicted and sentenced to hang.

Until now, he'd been delayed. First, by an illness that put him down for several days. Second, by a short spell behind the bars of a couple of Missouri county jails. Third, by a good deed that he'd done for a dying woman in the Cherokee Nation. Fourth, by a familial obligation to his mother and stepfather, Mary and Howard Loving.

This last detour from his goal turned out to be a blessing in disguise.

While cooling his heels in a Missouri jail, Creed received a letter from his sister Malinda, telling him that his mother and Howard were experiencing financial difficulties and that they needed his help. As soon as he was free again, Creed opted to return to Texas to aid them.

Creed assumed many of Howard's ranching duties, especially gathering the cattle and joining the stock with that of Howard's famous cousin, Oliver Loving, and cowman Charles Goodnight. With a crew of eighteen men that included Creed, Loving and Goodnight pushed their combined herd of two thousand head westward along the old Butterfield Stagecoach Road to the Pecos River, where they turned the beeves north to Fort Sumner and the Navajo Indian Reserve known as the Bosque Redondo.

On July 14, while they were camped on Las Carretas Creek north of Sumner, the partners decided to split up temporarily. Goodnight took three hands and returned to Texas with most of the money that the Army at Fort Sumner had paid them for their cattle; Loving pressed on with the remaining stock north to Colorado Territory. They agreed to join up again in the fall at the Bosque Redondo when Goodnight would arrive with another herd to be sold to the Army. Seeing the opportunity to pursue Marshall Quade before him, Creed chose to stay with Loving and drive the remainder of the first herd to Colorado.

With Creed to ramrod the outfit now, Loving pointed the herd of eight hundred head north, driving past Las Vegas and over the Raton Range. They crossed the Arkansas River near Pueblo and skirted the base of the Rockies to the vicinity of Denver with the idea that they would be able to sell the cattle in the mining districts, figuring that the miners would pay almost any price for a thick, juicy beefsteak.

Loving was well aware of this fact, and he drove hard bargains with every small-time buyer that approached him. When John Wesley Iliff came forward with an offer to buy the entire lot—all cows and calves that the Army had refused to buy in New Mexico—Loving leapt at the chance to dispose of the herd in one square deal, although he would be receiving a much lower price for the stock and despite Iliff's stipulation that required the Texans to deliver the cattle to his budding ranch north of Denver on the South Platte River.

Iliff invited Loving to be his guest for a few days. "Your men can recruit their horses and rest themselves," said the rancher. Loving hesitated to accept the offer because of the appointed rendezvous with Goodnight at Fort Sumner in the fall; the calendar already read August 12. In spite of Iliff's congenial insistence, Loving politely refused the invitation.

Some of Loving's drovers got wind of Iliff's invite, and the boss's declension sorely disappointed them. The thought of another hard ride straight back to New Mexico without a little rest and relaxation from the trail struck them as unfair, especially when they learned that Creed would be leaving them to look for Marshall Quade in Denver. The urge to sample a few of the temptations of the city caused a mild revolt among the men.

"Mr. Loving, we've been talking," said Tom Brooks, a former school teacher from east Texas, "and we were thinking that we'd like to spend some of our money down in Denver before going back to Sumner to meet Mr. Goodnight. There's not a whole lot of us here that's ever been to a place like that before. We'd kinda like to see what it's all about."

Loving didn't hold with his employees drinking and gambling when there was work to be done, and although they deserved some time to themselves, the thought of a dozen Texas drovers carousing the streets of Denver looking for a good time disturbed him. How much mischief could they find? he wondered. Maybe none, maybe a lot. No matter, though; he knew that he would have to grant their request or risk losing them altogether. He had to go to Denver anyway to find a bank where he could deposit most of the money that Iliff had paid him for the cattle. He had planned to take only Bose Ikard with him to carry the money, thinking that if any highwaymen should attempt to rob them, nobody would suspect a former slave of having a large amount of cash on him. But seeing the mood of the men, he relented, hoping that when he was ready to leave Denver they would be, too.

Loving had seen Denver before. On August 29, 1860, he and three other partners—Syl Reed, John Dawson, and Jowell Curtis—and their drovers trailed a herd north from Parker County, Texas, through the Indian nations to Kansas Territory until they struck the Arkansas River below the Great Bend. They followed that stream to Pueblo in that part of Kansas that would become Colorado Territory the following year, and they wintered the herd at a place north of the old Spanish town. When spring came and melted the snows, they drifted into Denver, peddled their cattle to miners and prospectors for top dollar, and prepared to return to Texas for another herd, but the outbreak of the War Between the States prevented them from leaving.

Loving finally managed to escape Denver in the summer of '61, crossing the Plains by stagecoach to St. Joseph, Missouri, where he was able to purchase a horse and ride back to Texas through the Indian nations. In time, the other Confederates also managed to leave Unionist Colorado for safer climes.

Denver didn't see any Texas drovers again until Loving and Creed returned with a trail crew August 16, 1866.

The outfit formed a fine procession as Creed and Loving led the crew through the streets of Denver, somewhat to the amusement of the citizenry. Texas drovers were as yet an unfamiliar curiosity in the city, one that provoked ladies to whisper and giggle and point and giggle some more, while gentlemen nudged each other in the ribs, pointed, and guffawed at their own moronic and sophomoric drolleries. The Texans ignored the curious stares and raucous laughter, choosing instead to place their attention on the buildings lining the street.

Named for General James W. Denver, the territorial governor when Colorado was still part of Kansas, Denver was a very young city, born on the banks of Cherry Creek where it flowed into the South Platte River. Still experiencing the labor pains of a premature birth in 1858, Denver merged in 1861 with its early neighbor, Auraria, a community established by William Green Russell, the discoverer of gold on nearby Little Dry Creek. Together, they fought off the challenges of other Colorado towns to become the territory's capital and the metropolis of the High Plains.

Fine homes and new businesses were springing up on every thoroughfare in Denver, as carpenters sawed their lumber and pounded their nails and as masons mixed their mortar and laid their bricks. Since the railroad was slow in reaching the territorial capital, teamsters raced everywhere, either delivering some commodity that was always in short supply or rushing back to the railhead in Nebraska for another load.

The drovers—the former slaves, Jim Fowler and Bose Ikard, in particular—were awed by every little thing. Never before had they seen so many people congregated at one time in one place. The speed with which everybody dashed about town astounded them. They wondered what pressing engagements caused these folk to hurry so.

And the noise! After the soundless breezes of the grasslands, broken only by the occasional bawling of the cattle, the pounding of hammers, the buzzing of saws, the rattling of wagons, and the shouts of men hard at work were deafening to the Texans' ears, imposing a reverent silence on them. Surely they would have turned tail and run had not one thought sustained them. Somewhere in that city was a saloon with warm beer, rotgut whiskey, crooked gaming tables, and friendly ladies of the evening just waiting for them and their money.

Loving turned his horse onto Blake Street, one of Denver's major thoroughfares. Straight ahead he saw a sign hanging out over the sidewalk designating the Rocky Mountain House. Beyond the hotel was the First National Bank of Denver. In the next block between F and E streets, the Elephant Corral stood out prominently among the business establishments there, and beside it was the Colorado House. Intrigued by the stable's moniker, he chose the Colorado. The hostelry appeared to be a respectable establishment, one quite suited to his tastes; and the bank being so near was convenient, too. He reined in his mount in front of the hotel, planning to tie it to the rail.

"Hold on a minute, Mr. Loving," said Brooks, his voice tinged with panic. "This place looks to be a mite too fancy for the likes of us. Maybe we'd better find us a hotel that's a little more fitting."

Loving scanned the faces of the drovers. "You may be right about that, Tom. You boys don't have to stay here if you don't want to. You each have your own money, so you can go where you please. Just remember one thing. The day after tomorrow at sunup, I'll be riding out of this town for New Mexico Territory. Those of you who want to remain in my employ will meet me here in front of this hotel at that time. If you're late, don't bother trying to catch up. Is that perfectly clear?"

Brooks spoke as if he were speaking for the entire crew. "Yessir, Mr. Loving. Sunup Monday morning. We'll be here, won't we, boys?"

A murmur of consent and a few nods from the drovers affirmed his question.

Satisfied, Loving waved them on their way, knowing full well that they were headed for a less reputable part of town. Nearly all of them turned their mounts and started looking for a good place to spend some of their well-earned pay. Creed,

Ikard, and Fowler remained with Loving.

"Why aren't you going with the others, Clete?" asked Loving. By way of being family, Loving naturally used Creed's real name, not his alias.

"This hotel will suit me just fine," said Creed.

"What about you two?"

"Jim and me figured you might need someone to help watch over things, Mr. Loving," said Ikard. His eyes shifted to the saddlebags hanging heavily over the croup of Loving's horse. "Leastways, till all that's in the proper place for it, sir."

"Yes, I see what you mean, Bose," said Loving. He patted the bags that held nearly all the gold that he had in the world, a fortune that would put him and his sons back on their financial feet. "Would you mind sharing a room with me, boys?" He shifted his weight to his left foot, swung his right leg over the gelding's haunches, and alit stiffly. Stretching, he noted that Ikard and Fowler hadn't moved to dismount. "What's wrong, boys?"

"Well, sir," said Ikard, "we wasn't planning on staying in the hotel with you. We was just thinking about watching over things till they's all in their proper place."

"You can do that, too," said Loving.

Ikard looked at Fowler for a second, then said, "You doesn't understand, Mr. Loving. We's Negroes."

Loving burped a laugh and said, "Hell, Bose, I can see that. I ain't blind, you know."

"No, Oliver," said Creed. "They're concerned about being allowed to stay here with you and me."

"I see," said Loving, turning serious again.

"Yes, sir," said Ikard. "We didn't think about staying in that there hotel with you, sir. We was thinking that after everything done been put in their proper place that we'd stay in the stable with the horses."

"Nonsense," said Loving. "There's nothing to worry about here. You're with me, and that's all that matters. Come on and get down, and let's go inside this hotel and see about some rooms. Come on now. Bose, you fetch my saddlebags with you."

"Yes, sir."

Creed, Ikard, and Fowler dismounted, tied up their horses, and took down their gear and bedrolls as well as Loving's. They followed Loving into the hotel.

The lobby was occupied by a half dozen men, each dressed stylishly in the latest of men's suits. The Texans appeared to be out of place in their linen dusters, denim trousers, leather chaps, colorful bandannas, high-heeled boots, and tall hats. The sight of them—their attire as well as their skin pigmentations—drew the attention of every person in the room, especially the desk clerk, who waited nervously for them to approach the registration counter.

Noting the indignant stares following the progress of the two ex-slaves, Creed said evenly, "Keep your heads up, men. You've got just as much right to be here as anybody."

Loving stepped up to the desk, took the pen to sign his name in the registry, and said, "We'll need two rooms for one night." He looked over his shoulder at Creed. "Will you need your room for more than one night, Clete?"

"I'll pay for my own room, Oliver."

"We're all filled up," said the clerk, his voice quavering and his aspect pale and fearful.

The Texas cowman replaced the pen in its holder and glowered at the shaking little man behind the counter. "All filled up, you say? I find that to be strange, sir, since I see so many keys hanging from those hooks behind you." He pointed at the rack on the wall behind the clerk.

"Those are extra keys, sir," said the clerk. Beads of perspiration were visible from his eyebrows to his receding hairline.

His fingers tapped a spasmodic rhythm on the desktop.

"I find that highly unlikely," said Creed, stepping forward and joining Loving at the counter.

"Sir, I don't think you understand the situation here," rejoined the clerk.

"I understand it perfectly," said Creed.

"And so do I," said Loving. "You are refusing me and my friends rooms in this hotel because these boys are Negroes. Isn't that it, sir?"

"Well, yes, sir, it is."

"At least you're honest about it," said Loving.

"Is there a problem here, Gibbons?" asked a man behind the Texans. They turned to see a tall gentleman with dark hair and a matching mustache standing a few feet away. Nattily dressed in a dark blue suit but neither carrying nor wearing a hat, the thirtyish fellow stepped forward with an air of exaggerated self-importance, which suggested that he might be the hotel's owner or merely the manager. He flashed an arrogant glance at Creed, then fixed an icy gaze on Loving. "Pardon me, sir, but might I inquire about where you . . . gentlemen . . . hail from?"

"Texas," said Loving.

"Texas, I see. Rebels, I suppose."

"We were Confederates, yes," said Loving, his eyebrows pinching together with anger. "What of it?"

"I know what he's getting at, Oliver," said Creed.

"What am I getting at, sir?"

Creed grinned benignly and said, "What's your name, mister? It wouldn't be asshole, would it?"

The man stiffened and growled, "Listen here, you Rebs. The war is over, and you lost. Evidently, you Texans aren't fully aware of that fact yet, and you don't seem to be aware of the fact that our late beloved President Lincoln freed the slaves."

Creed and Loving were incensed, but before either of them could react or speak, Ikard dropped Loving's saddlebags and other gear, stepped up to the gentleman, and said, "I ain't no slave, mister. I work for Mr. Loving by my own choice, and I get paid real good for it, too." He dug into a pants pocket and removed two double eagles. "See here at this money that's all mine? I earned it riding for Mr. Loving." He jammed the coins back into the pocket. "Now, if you don't mind, Mr. Loving and Mr. Creed has got business here in this hotel."

By now, every eye in the place was fixed on this little scene by the registration desk.

"No, they don't," said the gent indignantly. "As Gibbons said, we're all filled up right now."

"Pardon me, sir," said Loving, "but might I inquire about who you are and what your place is around here?"

"I am Edward Brown. I manage this fine establishment for my brother."

Creed set his saddlebags on the floor, unbuttoned his duster, then his coat as he moved closer to Brown. "I'd like you to take a look inside my coat, Mr. Brown," he said softly as he spread the garment apart just far enough for the manager to see the butt of the Colt's protruding ominously from his waistband. "I am from Texas, sir. I served three and a half years in the Confederate cavalry, and I fought in several battles throughout the South. I killed a lot of men in those years, and I've killed a few since then, but I haven't killed any hotel managers. Not yet, anyway."

Already pale and frightened by the gun, Brown flinched and mumbled, "You can't threaten me like that."

"Yes, I can. I'm doing it right now." He put his right hand on the grip of the Colt's. "Do we get those rooms, Mr. Brown, or do we find out if your hide is tough enough to stop a lead ball?"

Brown studied Creed for a sign that he was bluffing, but the Texan masked himself with the bland aspect of the Choctaw warrior confronting an enemy. Unable to read anything in Creed's face, the manager muttered, "I'll call the police and—"

Creed planted his left foot on the toe of Brown's right shoe and took the man's right arm in his left hand, interrupting the hotel official. Leaning closer to the manager, he whispered, "Dead men don't talk, Mr. Brown."

Fearful that Creed might carry out his threat, Loving stepped forward and said loudly, "A fine establishment you have here, Mr. Brown. I will recommend it to all my friends from Texas."

Brown looked past Creed and said, "Thank you, sir. We will certainly value their business."

"Fine," said Loving. "Now how about those rooms for my friends and me?"

"Gibbons, see that these gentlemen are cared for properly. Give them the best rooms in the house."

"Yes, sir, Mr. Brown." The desk clerk spun around to find the right keys for Loving and Creed. Taking them down from the rack, he did another about-face, placed the keys on the counter, and said, "That'll be two dollars a night for each room. Would you please sign the register, gentlemen?"

"You know, Mr. Brown," said Loving, "the manners of your employees are already improving around here." He took the pen and signed for himself, Ikard, and Fowler. "Do you want me to sign your name in here, Clete?"

"No, I'll take care of it, Oliver." He closed his coat and stepped up to put his name in the book. "We have four horses tied up out front. Is this hotel connected to that corral next door?"

"Yes, sir, we are," said Gibbons. "The stable is extra, of course."

"I'd expect it to be. Have our horses tended to right away then."

"Yes, sir."

Creed signed the book as Slate Creed, Double Star Ranch, Lavaca County, Texas.

Gibbons slid the keys across the counter to the Texans. "Here you are, gentlemen. Second floor and in the middle of the hall. Both rooms face the street."

Loving paid the man, snapped up the keys, and turned around to face the manager. "Yes, sir. Things are really improving around here already, Mr. Brown." He scanned the room. "Yes, sir, a very fine establishment. Shall we go, boys?" He started toward the stairway.

Creed picked up his saddlebags and said, "I'm glad your good sense came back to you, Mr. Brown. It would have been a shame to put a hole in that nice suit of yours." He walked past the manager and joined Loving on the first stair.

Ikard and Fowler picked up Loving's gear and followed them.

"Tell me, Clete," said Loving as they mounted the steps slowly. "Would you have shot that fool if he hadn't given us the rooms?"

Creed made no reply.

Loving understood. He didn't repeat the question.

4

After bathing and shaving, Creed brushed the trail dust from his hat and coat, unrolled his best trousers from his bedroll, and spit-shined his boots. He dressed as if he were planning to attend a cotillion that evening, but he wasn't. That was why he checked the loads in his Colt's before sticking it inside his waistband. All set now, he joined Loving, Ikard, and Fowler in the hall outside their rooms.

As a group, the four Texans descended the stairs, exited the hotel, and sauntered across the street to the First National Bank of Denver. Ikard and Fowler acted as guards while Loving deposited his money with David H. Moffat, the bank's cashier. Figuring he might be spending more than a few days in Denver, Creed decided to open an account with the bank. When that bit of business was concluded, the four walked outside to the boardwalk, unsure of what to do next.

"Well, I would like to see more of this city before it gets dark," said Loving as he surveyed first in one direction, then in the other. "You boys can either stay with me or you can find the rest of our outfit and join them in whatever merriment they might be up to by now."

"I'll walk with you a piece, Mr. Loving," said Fowler.

"I think I'll go look for Brooks and the others," said Creed. "If my guess is right, they've found a friendly saloon somewhere, and right now they're pouring down their first shots of courage before they go up to some lewd gal and ask her how much for her favors."

Loving chuckled and said, "I didn't think you went in for drinking and carousing, Clete."

"I don't anymore, but there was a time not long ago that I'd been right there with those boys when they rode off this morning. Too much water under the bridge since then, though, but I thought I'd just go see what they're up to and sort of make sure that they don't get into too much mischief."

"Good idea," said Loving. "What about you, Bose? Are you going with me or with Clete?"

"No offense, Mr. Loving, but going with Mr. Creed sounds like it'll be a lot more exciting than just seeing what the town looks like."

"I don't blame you, Bose. I admit that I'm almost tempted to go with him, too. Jim, are you thinking about changing your mind now that Bose has decided to go with Clete?"

"No, sir. I'm with you, Mr. Loving."

"Glad to have your company, Jim. All right, Clete. We'll see you and Bose back at the hotel, I suppose."

"Don't worry about us, Oliver. We'll be back before it gets too late."

Loving and Fowler headed off toward the stores on Blake Street, while Creed and Ikard drifted in the opposite direction, window shopping along the way, spying out everything from ladies' fashions to the newest rifles and handguns from back East. Denver was a curious sight to Ikard, but Ikard was an equally curious sight to Denver. Although most of the citizenry had seen Negroes at one time or another, few of them had ever met one or seen one wearing the garb of a Texas drover. Ikard was blissfully ignorant of this fact, but Creed wasn't. He was incensed by the stares and the cold conversations that they received from shop clerks and people on the streets. He figured, however, since Ikard seemed to be untouched by their offensive behavior that he, too, would ignore them.

When they passed the window of M. L. Rood's gun shop on F Street, Creed's eye was caught by a new rifle. He and Ikard entered the store to have a closer look at the weapon.

"Good afternoon, sir," said Rood, a bald, beardless, bespectacled man wearing garter sleeves and a work apron that was stained with gun oil. Rising from a stool at his workbench, he nodded at Ikard, which was more than most other people had done.

"Good afternoon," said Creed. "My friend and I were just passing by, and we noticed that rifle in your window."

"Yes, of course," said Rood, "the Winchester. It's a real eye-catcher all right." He stepped over to a rack of Winchesters on the wall, took one down, and handed it to Creed. "It's the new .44-caliber. It's an improvement on the Henry repeater. It's got a new magazine mechanism that makes it easier to load the cartridge into the chamber."

Creed hefted the gun. "It certainly feels like a Henry, but you say it works better than the Henry?"

"Yes, sir, it does. I take it you already have a Henry, Mr.—?"

"Creed. Slate Creed, and my friend here is Bose Ikard. We're from Texas."

"Ah, yes. You must be part of that cattle outfit that I read about in the newspaper. The one that just delivered a herd of cows to Mr. Iliff on his ranch?"

"Yes, we're part of that outfit," said Creed.

"Being from Texas, you must really know firearms, Mr. Creed. Did you fight in the war?"

"Cavalry," said Creed. Then anticipating Rood's next question, he added, "Confederate."

"Well, the war is over, isn't it, Mr. Creed?"

Creed studied Rood for a second, looking for sincerity in the man's eyes. Finding some, he said, "Yes, it is, and now folks like my friend here are free to live their own lives as they see fit." The last he added as another test.

"As they should have been from birth," said Rood quite seriously. "But I suppose there were those who held other views."

"Sad to say, Mr. Rood, there were, and they nearly got me killed a few times fighting for them. To be honest about it, sir, I now resent them for it."

"Those were unhappy times, but now they are in the past. We can only hope that everybody learns from them, and we can move ahead as one people now."

"Amen," said Creed. "Now about this Winchester. Is there a place where I can try it out?"

Rood smiled and said, "Sadly, no, not in the city. The law forbids the use of firearms within the corporation limits." He had an idea. "When are you leaving town, Mr. Creed?"

"I don't know. I have business here that could keep me here several days, maybe even a few weeks."

"Well, sir, you strike me as an honest man, and I hope you think of me in the same vein. With that thought in mind, I will make you this offer. You take that Winchester with you now, Mr. Creed, and try it out. Outside the city, of course. And if you like it, then good, you have a new rifle. If you don't like it, bring it back, and I will refund your money cheerfully. How does that strike you?"

"It sounds like I can't lose on a deal like that, Mr. Rood. What do you think, Bose?"

"Sounds good to me, Mr. Creed," said Ikard.

"All right then, Mr. Rood, I'll take it." He handed the rifle to the gunsmith. "I'll be back on Monday to pay for it."

"Would you like to make your Henry part of the purchase price, Mr. Creed?" asked Rood.

"Good idea. What would I do with two rifles?" He glanced
at Ikard and saw a touch of anxiety in his eyes. "On second
thought, Mr. Rood, I think I'll just pay cash for the Winchester. Bose, you need a good rifle. How about I make you a
present of my Henry?"

"No sir, Mr. Creed. I got money to pay for it. I'd be pleased
to buy it from you."

"Fair enough," said Creed. "Mr. Rood, what were you
planning to give me for my Henry?"

Rood pinched his chin between index finger and thumb
as he gave Creed's question some thought. "Maybe fifteen
dollars?"

"Not a bad price," said Creed. "How does that sound to
you, Bose? Fifteen dollars for my Henry."

Ikard beamed a joyous smile and said, "Sounds just about
right to me, Mr. Creed."

"Then it's done. Bose will buy my Henry, and I'll be back
on Monday morning to buy that fine Winchester from you,
Mr. Rood. Fair enough?"

"Fair enough," said Rood. Before the Texans could turn
and leave, he added nervously, "Mr. Creed, might I inquire
about your handgun?"

"My handgun?"

"Yes, sir. The one in your trousers."

Creed smiled and said, "I always hope that nobody will
notice that I'm armed, but I suppose a gunsmith would be
paying close attention to such things."

"A gunsmith and . . . a policeman, Mr. Creed. Especially
since you gentlemen are from Texas."

"I see your point, Mr. Rood." Creed unbuttoned his coat and
drew the gun from his waistband. Hefting it with respect and
appreciation, he spoke reverently about the weapon. "Colt's
.44 cap-and-ball revolver, Mr. Rood. It's served me well ever
since it came to be mine last year." He remembered seeing

the gun for the first time two Mays ago in John Kelly's store
back home in Hallettsville. All shiny and new, never fired,
he had looked on it as his even before he bought it, and since
then, although several attempts had been made to separate
him from it, the gun had been his constant and dependable
companion. "Whenever I've had to shoot it at a man, it's
been true and deadly. You might say it's saved my life on
more than one occasion."

"Have you killed many men with it, Mr. Creed?" asked
Rood cautiously.

"That's a score I don't keep, Mr. Rood. Let me just say
that the number is more than I care to think about."

"Yes, sir, I see," said Rood. A brief silence followed before
he added, "Well, I was wondering about your handgun because
several men have brought their cap-and-ball pistols to me for
conversion to cartridge firing."

"You can do that?"

"Yes, sir. It's simply a matter of removing the nipples and
boring through the cylinder to allow you to load the cartridges
into it. And, of course, I have to replace the hammer."

Creed studied the gun in his hand and wondered about
all the newfangled improvements in revolvers and ammunition. He knew of several variations of the Colt's .44-caliber
percussion revolver, including the metallic cartridge versions
produced by the Smith & Wesson company, and he'd heard
many bad things about them, especially the reports that the
metallic cartridges were often unreliable, that they frequently
failed to fire immediately, if at all, and that the only way of
testing them was to shoot off several rounds from a box and
hope that the remaining loads were reliable. For a man who'd
had his life challenged more times than he cared to remember,
undependable ammunition would never do.

"Well, Mr. Rood, it's like this," said Creed. "Unless you
can guarantee that the cartridges I put in the cylinder are

gonna fire every time I squeeze the trigger, I don't believe I'll have my gun converted."

"I can't do that, Mr. Creed."

"That's what I thought. No offense intended, Mr. Rood. It's just that I have to know that my gun is gonna shoot when I squeeze the trigger because most likely my life will be depending on it."

Rood was speechless for the moment, stunned that a young man like Creed, with obvious intelligence and natural charm, could speak so unemotionally about killing other men, that he could talk about it in the same dull tone that a mechanic would use to describe the internal workings of a complicated machine. He'd heard several former soldiers, especially those militiamen who'd served under Colonel Chivington at Sand Creek, tell how they'd killed Indians or Confederates, and he'd been sickened by their descriptions of the gore. This was different. Whereas the braggarts had shown disgusting delight in taking human life, Creed was displaying all the morbidity of an undertaker preparing his five hundredth body for burial.

Rood's lack of a response surprised Creed for a second before he realized how he must have sounded to the gunsmith. Damn! he thought. Why'd I go and say that? I've scared this poor man shitless. How do I fix that now?

"Well, thank you for the offer to convert my Colt's, Mr. Rood," said Creed awkwardly, "but I believe I'll pass."

Rood swallowed the lump in his throat and said, "Why did you call your gun a Colt's, Mr. Creed?"

This question also caught Creed by surprise. "I don't know," he said. "That's all I've ever called it. In fact, that's all I've ever heard it called back in Texas. From my earliest childhood days, I've never heard it called anything except Mr. Colt's revolver, Colt's revolver, and just a Colt's." A memory came to mind. "I recollect when my daddy brought home a pair of them back at the start of the last war with Mexico."

"The last war with Mexico?" queried Rood. "There's only been one war with Mexico."

"Maybe for the United States," said Creed, "but not for Texas. We Texans fought Mexico three times."

"Yes, of course," said Rood. "Just like the United States had to fight England twice."

"Exactly," said Creed. "Anyway, my daddy brought a pair home with him, and then he rode off to defend the frontier against the Comanches." He turned sad and added, "They killed him and took his guns. I was only five years old, but I've wanted to get those guns back ever since then." He stared at the Colt's for a moment before making an observation. "Strange, isn't it, how the oddest things stir up memories that you haven't thought about for years?" When neither of the other two men spoke, Creed found the volume of their silence to be deafening. He chuckled purposely and said, "Will you listen to me now? You know, Bose, a man I know has told me more than once that I spend too much time in the pulpit. Do you think he's right?"

"Could be, Mr. Creed," said Ikard with a forced smile.

"Well, I suppose we should be on our way," said Creed. He shoved the revolver inside his waistband again. "We have friends to find." He realized that he didn't have the vaguest idea about where they should begin looking for Brooks and the other drovers. "Mr. Rood, if you were a Texas drover new in town, where would you go to find some bad whiskey, a lewd woman, and a game of cards or dice?"

"Across the creek in Auraria. The Rocky Mountain, the Chicago, or the Baltimore. On Fourth Street. You can probably find your friends in that section of town. Just go back to Blake Street, turn right, and follow it across the bridge. Fourth Street is a block south on the other side of Cherry Creek."

"Thank you, Mr. Rood. I'll be back on Monday to pick up the Winchester. Good afternoon, sir."

Rood bid them farewell and watched them leave. He went to the door to put up the *Closed* sign and pull the shade. His eyes followed the two Texans as they walked along the boardwalk toward Blake Street. Such an unusual fellow, he thought. I wonder if I'll ever see him again.

5

The first gold rush to Colorado was started in July 1858 when a band of Georgians led by William Green Russell went prospecting in wild Indian country and found gold. News of their discovery of a small placer on Little Dry Creek, a tributary of the South Platte River, stimulated enough imaginations to set the wildest rumors afloat on the prairie wind. A succession of prospecting parties hastened westward across the vast Plains as fast as the tales of incredible riches reached the East. During the fall and winter of that year, the population along the South Platte grew daily as men from every state and territory poured into the valley in search of gold, Mostly, these immigrants chose to settle beneath the cottonwoods at the juncture of Cherry Creek and the South Platte. Two little towns sprang up here: Auraria and Denver City.

Russell and his brothers, Oliver and Levi, named Auraria after their Georgia home. Another group of settlers platted Denver City on the plot of ground where an earlier group had staked out the town of St. Charles, renaming it for the territorial governor with the hope that he would favor it in dealing with that region of Kansas Territory. Their hopes did not go unrewarded. Governor Denver ordered the formation of Arapahoe County, and he designated Denver City as the county seat, giving the community a permanence that the land speculators of other settlements envied greedily.

One of the last acts of President James Buchanan was the signing of the bill that gave Kansas statehood and that authorized the formation of Colorado Territory in February 1861 with Denver as its capital. Denver continued to grow as it became the receiving, warehouse, and distribution center for the mining towns in the mountains to the west and the farming and ranching communities along the rivers to the north, south, and east.

Before marrying into one city, Auraria and Denver City lived as differently as a man and a woman. Many of Auraria's original settlers left the village soon after the major discoveries of gold in the mountains, while Denver City's founders, led by General William Larimer and newspaperman William Byers, publisher and editor of *The Rocky Mountain News,* stayed and established a stable community. A lesser class element moved into Auraria, while Byers and Larimer attracted the more stable people then migrating to Colorado Territory. Auraria developed a notoriety, and Denver City nurtured a touch of prestige.

After the merger of the twin towns on Cherry Creek, thanks largely to Byers, the new city of Denver inherited the good and the bad of its two predecessors. The good included the strongest business and banking institutions in the South Platte River Valley, and the bad consisted of some of the raunchiest saloons, gambling dens, and bawdy houses between St. Louis and San Francisco. For the first few years, the city fathers directed the orderly growth of Denver, and they contained the less reputable concerns to the west bank of Cherry Creek in old Auraria, now West Denver. Some thought this frontier Sodom and Gomorrah south of the creek would have its day, then be dealt a deathblow by the hand of Providence. They almost got their wish.

Most of Denver was quiet and asleep at two o'clock in the morning of April 19, 1863. Little noise could be heard above the high winds that had been sweeping across the Plains from the Rockies for several days. Along Blake Street near F Street, the wind muffled the noise of late tipplers in the drinking establishments, and nobody heard the first cries of *"Fire!"* when a careless reveler kicked over a stove at the Cherokee House.

Soon piercing screams giving the warning broke the early morning peace, and sleepers on both sides of Cherry Creek came awake with consternation and fear. The harsh winds proved to be a mixed blessing as the flames grew brighter in the vicinity of the Cherokee House. The blow's eastward direction from the mountains prevented the fire from spreading to the west side of the creek, but it swirled sparks and burning debris all over the heart of the eastern sector of Denver. Flames quickly consumed the hastily constructed frame buildings, and they gutted the more recently built brick buildings. Within a few hours, most of East Denver between Cherry Creek, Wazee, and G Street lay in blackened ruins.

The Great Fire, as the locals were calling the conflagration when Loving, Creed, and the other Texans arrived in Denver, did an estimated $350,000 worth of damage. It left scores of people homeless, and the destruction crippled or ruined more than two dozen businesses. Despite the fact that few people had insurance, many had a reason to be thankful: nobody died in the fire.

No sooner had Denver been rebuilt bigger and better than another disaster changed the face of the town. Exactly thirteen months to the day after The Great Fire, the hand of Providence slapped the unsuspecting community with even greater ferocity. For several years, local Indians and old mountain men warned the townsmen that idle streambeds such as Cherry Creek sometimes behaved violently when heavy rains fell in the mountains, but the greenhorns observed that Cherry Creek seldom carried more than a small rivulet of water, even during the spring melt and seasonal showers. Ignoring sage wisdom, builders jammed both banks of Cherry Creek with stores, shops, and warehouses, while some buildings such as city hall and the Trinity Methodist Church were constructed in the creek bed itself.

For a week prior to May 19, 1864, unusually steady and heavy rains poured on the mountains and Plains to the south of Denver. On the afternoon of May 19 a shower struck the city. When the rain stopped, black clouds continued to engulf the region, clouds so dense that the mountains were obscured for hours. That evening a few people noticed that Cherry Creek ran higher than usual, but nobody expressed any alarm or concern. Just before midnight most Denverites were snuggled in bed, while the pleasure seekers filled the gambling halls, saloons, and bawdy houses as usual.

All had their night disrupted by a strange sound approaching from the south. The noise possessed the resonance of a strong wind blowing through a pine forest. It increased gradually and steadily to a mighty roar as a great wall of water, bearing on its crest trees and other drift, rushed toward the settlement. Unlike the fire of the previous year, the flood gave no warning as it spread. This time Auraria, now West Denver, wasn't spared. The citizenry was wrenched from peaceful slumber by the terrifying roar of destruction, and hundreds of people were forced to flee their homes for safety. Those most affected by the flood were the residents who had foolishly built on the flood plain of the creek, thinking that they would be safe from the spring overflows if they placed their houses and businesses on stilts. This precaution availed them nothing. Even the imposing edifice of *The Rocky Mountain News* building was swept away with the shoddily built saloons and bawdy houses on the opposite bank.

After the flood, only a few dens of iniquity remained in West Denver. Rood, the gunsmith, in talking with Creed, had mentioned three of these: "Stout Tom" Mundy's Baltimore and Billy Morton's Chicago on Fourth Street between Front and Cherry Streets, and Johnny Moore's Rocky Mountain Saloon on Blake Street between the creek and Front Street.

Creed and Ikard crossed the Blake Street bridge to West Denver and quickly found the Rocky Mountain, but none of their friends were there. They walked the block over to Fourth Street and its declining tenderloin district. This wasn't exactly Creed's kind of place, and it definitely wasn't Ikard's. With cautious apprehension, they moved along the boardwalk until they came to the Baltimore Saloon. Creed peeked through the open door, hoping to see a familiar face, but he saw none. They went on to the Chicago.

Creed opened the glass-paneled door and stepped inside the saloon. Customers from several occupations—miners, teamsters, draymen, ranch and farm hands, Texas drovers, and laborers for every trade—filled the room. A handful of the district's preying denizens—pick-pockets, blackleg gamblers, confidence artists, footpads, and other such petty thieves—peppered the hall, looking and acting colorful, for the entertainment of the paying patrons and for their own benefit. Mingling among the men were a half dozen barmaids attired in dresses that exposed their blue-stockinged calves and ankles. A heavy cloud of ghostly tobacco smoke hung in the air above the imbibers. The long oak bar dominated the left side of the room, and a staircase ran up the other wall to private rooms on the second story of the frame building. A few round tables with six wing chairs each occupied the remaining floor space. A man armed with a double-barrel shotgun and a revolver sat on a tall stool guarding a door to the illegal gaming room in the rear.

"Slate!" called out Tom Brooks.

With twilight beginning to settle over the land, Creed had little difficulty adjusting his vision to the dim light of the watering hole. He recognized Brooks leaning against the bar, a shot glass in his hand, a blue bottle of Old Taos in front of him. "There's Tom," he said over his shoulder to Ikard.

"Come on over here and let me buy y'all a drink," said Brooks. He spotted Ikard and added, "You, too, Bose. I especially want to buy you a drink. Bartender, set 'em up for my boss and the best damn drover in Texas."

Creed and Ikard joined Brooks at the rail, and Creed ordered beer for them.

The bardog, a stout fellow with slicked-down brown hair and a waxed longhorn mustache, glared at Ikard and declared, "We don't serve coloreds at the bar."

"Where do you serve them?" asked Creed evenly, trying to contain his anger at the bartender's attitude.

"In the back."

Creed turned and spotted the guard with the shotgun on his lap. "Through that door?"

"No, not in there," said the bartender indignantly. "Just in the back of the room."

"All right," said Creed. "We'll have two beers, and we'll have them back there."

"You're not gonna drink with him, are you?" inquired the barman, astounded that a white man would socialize with a former slave. Such decency was unheard of in Denver.

Creed fixed his gaze on the man's dull brown eyes and said, "Wouldn't you drink with a man who saved your life?"

"Well, sure," said the bartender. He shifted his view to Ikard and added, "But he's colored," as if Creed and Brooks hadn't noticed Ikard's skin pigmentation.

"You know, mister," said Brooks, "when Bose here was saving our hides from a herd of stampeding longhorns, I didn't stop to notice that his skin was darker than mine, and I don't think it entered his mind neither. Slate and me and the others who were in camp when those cattle took to running owe our lives to this man." He draped an arm around Ikard's shoulders. "He really deserves to stand right here and drink with us. In fact, we're the ones who should be honored to drink with him. Ain't that right, Slate?"

"That's right, Tom." Creed fixed a determined stare on the bartender and said, "Now how about those beers, mister?"

"Aw, hell," said the bardog. "You might as well drink them right here if he's such a hero." He drew two foamy mugs of lager and set them down in front of the Texans. "That'll be four bits."

"Take it outta here," said Brooks, sliding a silver dollar across the countertop. "Drink up, Bose." Brooks raised his glass in toast. The odor of his breath and the glaze in his eyes said that this wasn't his first drink; it was probably his eighth or ninth.

The three of them clinked glasses.

"To Texas!" said Brooks.

"To Texas!" said Creed and Ikard simultaneously.

Brooks tipped his head back and threw the shot of whiskey down his gullet.

Ikard watched Creed blow the head from his beer, then he tried it. The result wasn't quite the same. Ikard lacked Creed's finesse and experience as the foam sprayed off the mug and plopped onto the floor instead of spreading itself over the rim of the glass and dripping to the floor. He took a long draw on the beer, then wiped his mouth on his sleeve.

After taking a healthy swallow of the brew, Creed put his glass on the bar and turned to survey the people in the room. The barmaids caught his attention immediately as they passed through the noisy crowd serving beer and liquor to the men, while adroitly avoiding the pinches, pats, and grabs of their customers' eager hands. Four of the females were brunettes with pleasing features, but none of them stood out from the others. The fifth was a blonde with the whitest skin that he had ever seen and blue eyes that fairly sparkled above her rouged cheeks. She was attractive, and in a way, she reminded Creed of the girl who was still waiting for him back in Texas. He sighed wistfully.

"Which one would you go for, Slate?" asked Brooks. "How about that pretty blonde? Is she anything like that girl of yours back in Texas?"

Creed turned around to his beer, ignoring the question because he didn't like the idea of anybody ogling Texada or even a woman who looked like her.

Brooks, like all the men who had shared two and a half months on the trail with Creed, knew about Texada, knew about Creed's trouble with the Federals, knew about his adventures since leaving Lavaca County. Also like the other men, he was sympathetic to Creed and would do almost anything to help Creed prove his innocence and regain the life that was rightfully his. Seeing Creed's reaction to his question, he felt a little guilt that was intensified by the alcohol that he'd consumed. "Sorry about that, Slate," he said.

Creed took a draw on his beer, swallowed hard, and sighed again. He turned to Brooks and said, "You shouldn't be sorry, Tom. I'm the one who ought to apologize to you for behaving like that." He scanned the crowd again and focused on the blonde. "Yes, she does remind me a bit of Texada. Her hair isn't quite as golden as Texada's, and I don't think Texada's skin was that white even on the day she was born." Then thinking to soften the moment even more, he added, "Does looking at her put a knot in your gut, Tom?"

"Well, I kinda like that black-haired gal over there in the corner," said Brooks. "She looks a little like a Mexican gal I met once."

At the mention of Mexican girls, an image of Silveria Abeytia flashed into Creed's mind, and he felt another tug at his heart strings. If he hadn't already promised himself to Texada, he would have fulfilled his desire to be with Silveria. She was so beautiful, he thought. I could have stayed in Mexico and—Aw, damn! To hell with that kind of thinking. You can't do anything until you do something about that noose hanging over your head.

He took another swallow of beer before he finally saw the raven-haired girl that Brooks had mentioned. Even in the poor light and the haze of smoke, he recognized something familiar about her. He couldn't be sure, but something said she was a tie to home, to Texas, to Lavaca County, to—*Glengarry!*

"I think I know that girl," said Creed softly.

"What's that you say, Slate?" asked Brooks.

"I think I know her," he said louder. He put his beer down on the bar and headed off through the crowd.

"Could you introduce me to her, Slate?" asked Brooks eagerly as he started to follow Creed, only to stop when he saw that he might lose his place at the rail. "Bring her back with you, Slate. We'll wait here. Won't we, Bose?"

Creed didn't hear Ikard's reply as he weaved through the tables to the black-haired girl serving a table of teamsters and a sport who seemed to be holding court. As he drew closer, his mind swirled with memories of those happier years in his life, the years before the war when his grandfather Dougald Slater was still alive, full of living, and in charge of everything, including the lives of his grandchildren, his daughter-in-law, and his slaves.

Glengarry Plantation was an idyllic place except for one circumstance—slavery. Although the Slater slaves were the healthiest and happiest in Texas, they were still slaves, bound to their master from birth. Dougald Slater told them on more than one occasion: "You're free to leave here anytime you want. I'll even give you the papers that make you free. But where would you go and what would you do if I did set you free? Would you go north? How would you get there? Walk?

You'd starve before you got there. Would you stay around here? Or stay in Texas? You'd starve here as well because no white Texan would give you work unless you become his slaves. If you went somewhere else in the South, you might make it before you starve, and when you did, you'd be faced with much the same problem that you have here in Texas. Go if you want, but think about it before you do." They thought about it, and they stayed. They stayed as long as Dougald Slater was alive. When he died, he set them free in his will. Some left then, but the rest remained until the Federal soldiers arrived in Lavaca County to set them free at last.

Among the latter was Dinah. Before becoming Slater chattel, she was a house servant on an east Texas plantation where she gave birth to three children, all three of them being the offspring of the master's oldest son. When the son married, his new bride insisted that his nigger whore and her whelps should be sold South. Dougald Slater bought the whole family at the slave market in Houston because he needed another maid for his new mansion and because his grandchildren needed playmates and Dinah's children were approximately the same ages as Clete, Malinda, and Dent.

Soon after coming to Glengarry, Dinah married another Slater slave, and they had their own family. When the presence of Union soldiers guaranteed their freedom and travel seemed relatively safe, Dinah gathered her family about her and declared that they were leaving for Kansas immediately. All but her second oldest daughter, Hannah, eagerly agreed to go. All except Dinah tried to dissuade the stubborn child from staying. Dinah knew Hannah's reason for remaining. She didn't like it, but she understood and let her stay.

Hannah left the plantation in time, too, and now Creed stood only a few feet from her. The former slave at Glengarry possessed a natural earthy beauty: amber skin that was unblemished, jet black hair that was soft and silky to the eye as well as to the touch, almond eyes that could be alluring in one instant and filled with motherly love in the next, enticing lips that appeared to be stained with elderberry wine and that begged to be kissed, and a form that was lithe and gently curved and that moved with a grace so sensuous that few men would escape the flames it could fan in their loins. She glanced up at Creed, offered him a fleeting smile, then resumed serving the beers to her customers, paying him no more attention than she would any stranger. As soon as she put the last mug on the table, she gave Creed another cursory scan, then started toward the bar, only to stop and study his face for a moment. Disbelief then fear painted her features.

Creed smiled at her and queried, "Hannah?"

"No comprendo, señor," she said.

"¿No comprendo?" repeated Creed. "What?" Confusion pinched his eyebrows together. He thought he recognized the voice as being Hannah's, but it had been so long since he'd last seen her. When was that? he wondered. Briefly at Glengarry last year? No, but she was there—I think.

The girl averted her eyes and moved away toward the bar again.

"Hey, wait a minute," said Creed as he followed her. "I want to talk to you."

"No comprendo, señor," she said as she darted behind the security of the bar.

Creed would have gone behind the bar after her, but somebody grabbed him by the arm and stopped him. He spun around to see the sport who had been holding court at the table where the girl had been serving.

"Just hold on there, friend," said the swell. He wore a navy blue suit and vest with charcoal pinstripes, a boiled shirt, and a maroon cravat with a rhinestone pin.

Creed glared at the hand on his arm, noting a gold and rhinestone ring on the pinky finger. He shifted his view to the fellow's face: blue eyes, a wisp of brown mustache, pale complexion, and a sneer of arrogance. Looking him up and down at his tall, narrow frame, Creed judged the fellow to be close to reaching his majority, although not quite there yet. He wrenched his arm free.

"The girl said, '*No comprendo,*' friend. Or don't you understand Mex?"

With iron in his eyes and ice in his voice, Creed said, "*Yo entiendo español muy bueno, muchacho. ¿Y tu? ¿Cuánto sabes tu, cabrón?*"

The swell's upper lip quivered in anger.

Men close to them ceased their conversations and turned their attention to the vignette unfolding before them.

"What are you, mister?" the swell finally managed to stutter. "Some sort of wise ass?"

Creed's Choctaw ancestry came to the fore as he allowed his features to go stony while his left hand unbuttoned his coat. "You may apologize for that remark, sir," he said, "and I won't demand satisfaction."

"Apologize?" growled the sport. "Do you know who you're talking to?"

The room had grown quiet as everybody focused on Creed and his antagonist.

"Frankly, I don't give a damn who you are," said Creed as he casually took hold of the left flap of his coat, while his eyes kept a steady bead on the swell. "You owe me an apology, and you've got less than a minute to make it."

The ominous CLICK-CLICK! of twin gun hammers being cocked into firing position split the air like lightning parting clouds, paralyzing most of the crowd into fearful silence.

"I got both barrels trained on you, mister," said the guard at the door to the gaming room. "I'll cut you in two if you reach for that pistol under your coat."

Creed refused to shift his eyes or even to blink.

The sport sputtered, "You were gonna draw on me?"

"Easy, Jimmy," said the guard. "You know Billy don't hold with gunfighting in here. If you want to shoot it out with this fellow, then you can just take your fight outside, you hear?"

"Did you hear what he called me, Bob?" whined Jimmy. "Cabrón—a bastard."

"I heard him, but that don't make any difference. If you want to fight, take it outside."

"Naw, I think I'll just whip his ass right here." He threw a punch that Creed blocked easily with his left forearm.

"Jimmy!" snapped Bob.

Out of the corner of his eye, Creed saw the guard change the aim of the shotgun as he jumped down from the stool. This was his opening. He kicked his right boot into Jimmy's crotch, catching him in the balls with the top of his foot and lifting Jimmy a good six inches off the floor.

Jimmy let out a tiny peep of pain when he came down, then he grabbed his groin and dropped to his knees in agony. His sallow face purpled as he gasped for air and his eyes bulged.

In the same instant, Creed dodged to the side until Jimmy was between him and the guard. He drew his Colt's, cocked it, and put the muzzle to Jimmy's head.

Bob leveled his shotgun at Creed.

Every man near Creed and Jimmy scattered, trying to get out of the guard's line of fire.

"Go ahead and try your luck, friend," said Creed, "You might kill me, but I'll kill him first, and I'll take you out, too, before I hit the floor."

"That's mighty tall talk, mister," said Bob.

"Not where I come from."

"And where might you come from?"

"Texas."

"A Reb?"

"An American," said Creed with pride and finality.

Silence.

Jimmy caught his breath. "Jesus, Bob, don't let him kill me," he blubbered.

"He's not gonna kill you, Jimmy," said Bob.

"I won't if you don't force my hand," said Creed.

"You don't have to worry about that, mister," said Bob as he aimed the shotgun at the ceiling and eased back on the twin hammers.

The door to the gaming room opened, and a short, portly gent with red hair, full red beard and mustache, stormy eyes emerged. "What's going on here, Stockton?" he demanded. He scanned the room until his view fell on Jimmy and Creed. "What's that all about now? What's Jimmy doing on the floor?"

"The Texan put him there, Mr. Morton," said Bob Stockton.

"The Texan?"

"Yes, sir. That fellow with the gun in his hand."

"Jimmy picked another fight, did he?" asked Morton.

"Yes, sir, he did."

"Throw both of them out."

"No, sir," said Creed, still holding the muzzle of his Colt's to Jimmy's head. "I have done nothing to warrant such treatment."

"You were part of a fight in my saloon, mister," said Morton, "and that's plenty of reason to have you thrown out of here. Now you can either go—"

"No, sir," interjected Creed. "I came in here minding my own business and planning to have a quiet little drink with my friends. I haven't finished that drink yet."

"All right," said Morton, "finish your drink, then get the hell out of my saloon. Stockton, get your brother out of here."

"Why do I have to go?" whined Jimmy. "I didn't do nothing. This . . ." He thought of calling Creed some foul name, but the Colt's deterred him. " . . . this Texan started it by bothering Juanita."

"Juanita?" queried Morton. He scanned the room until his view fell on the girl cowering behind the bar. "Was he bothering you, Juanita?"

"*No, señor,*" she said honestly.

"I only wanted to talk to the girl," said Creed, "but this fellow butted in when he shouldn't have."

"Is that what happened, Stockton?" asked Morton.

"That's pretty much how it went, Mr. Morton."

Morton twisted up his lips as he considered what he should do next. He heaved a sigh and said, "Stockton, throw your brother out of here."

"But, Mr. Morton—" pleaded Jimmy.

"Shut your mouth, Jimmy!" snapped Stockton. He stomped across the room, grabbed his brother by an arm, and jerked him to his feet. "Get your hat and get the hell out of here. You've caused enough trouble for one day."

As soon as Jimmy was out the door, Morton turned to Creed and said, "Mister, my apologies for the trouble. I thank you for not shooting up the place. Have a drink on me, if you please."

Creed uncocked his revolver, replaced it inside his waistband, and said, "Thank you kindly, sir. I will."

"Juanita, you serve that man whatever he wants," said Morton, giving the girl a hard look, "and I do mean whatever he wants."

"*Sí, señor.*"

"All right, gents," said Morton, "the fuss is over. You can go back to your drinking now."

The room became noisy again as Stockton led his brother to the door, Morton went back into the gaming room, and

Creed stepped up to the bar where the girl waited nervously for him.

"¿Te llamas Juanita?" asked Creed with a smile that was meant to set her at ease.

The girl's brow twisted slightly as if she were trying to figure out what it was that Creed had just said to her. When she made the translation in her mind, she smiled anxiously and said, "Sí, me llamo Juanita."

"!Muy bien, Juanita, muy bien!" He looked down the bar at Brooks and Ikard, then back at the girl. "Mis amigos. Somos Tejanos. ¿Y tu? ¿Eres Tejana?"

Her almond eyes bugged for a second with fear, then she averted them.

"That's what I thought," said Creed softly. When she looked up at him again, he added, "Why don't we go somewhere we can talk nice and private, Juanita?" He surveyed the room for a place where they could talk, but he didn't see one.

The girl took his hand and said, "Come with me." She pulled him toward the staircase.

Brooks and Ikard watched them go.

"Now will you look at that?" said Brooks. "I ask him to introduce me to that gal, and he goes off with her himself. Now if that don't beat all."

"Maybe Mr. Slate is just gonna try her out and see if she's good enough for you, Mr. Tom," said Ikard.

"Maybe so, Bose." Brooks watched wistfully until Creed and the girl disappeared at the top of the stairs. He turned back to his whiskey and said, "Hell, I guess seconds is better than no woman at all."

6

The girl led Creed through the upstairs hall to a door halfway to the end. She opened it and stepped into a dark room that had a single window overlooking the back lot of the saloon.

Creed hesitated to follow her inside until she had lit a lamp on a chest of drawers at the long end of the space that measured a scant eight feet by ten feet. He noted that the only other pieces of furniture in the room were an infant's cradle and a bed that was barely big enough to accommodate two average-size people lying side by side. He closed the door behind him and turned to the girl who stood cowering in the corner next to the bureau. "You are Hannah, aren't you?"

She lowered her frightened eyes and said, "Yes, sir, Mr. Clete, I am."

"Look at me, Hannah." His tone was parental. He waited for her to look up. "You're not a slave now. You don't have to look at the ground when you talk to white people, and you sure as hell don't have to look at the floor when you talk to me."

"Yes, sir."

"And none of that sir business." He smiled. "Good lord, Hannah, we grew up together. You never called me sir when we were living at Glengarry, and I don't want you to start now."

"Yes, sir, uh, I mean, Mr. Clete."

"And no more of that Mr. Clete business. You can call me Clete or you can call me Slate. It makes no difference to me. Whichever one you prefer."

"Slate? Is that short for Slater?" she asked.

"Yes, it is. I go by the name of Slate Creed now."

"You do? Why?"

"You don't know?"

"No, sir, uh, I mean . . ." Catching herself again, she determined that she wouldn't make the mistake again, that she would accede to his wishes and speak to him as an equal. "No, I don't know, Clete."

"Well, it's a long story, but I'd rather find out a few things about you first. Like, what are you doing here in Denver and in a place like this? And what was all that business downstairs with the Mexican talk?"

"Like you said, Clete, it's a long story."

Creed dropped onto the bed, leaned back on an elbow, and said, "How much is your time gonna cost me?"

Hannah didn't quite understand immediately, but when she figured out what he meant, she said, "Two dollars, but that's for one time. If you want me for longer than that, it's five dollars. Ten dollars for the whole night."

"I got the money." He dug in the coin pocket of his trousers, fished out a double eagle, and tossed it on the bed. "Now you give me the time."

Hannah bolted the door, then sat down on the opposite end of the bed out of Creed's immediate reach, not that he had indicated that he wanted to touch her, but just to keep the proper distance that she felt was necessary, all things considered. "I don't rightly know where to start," she said.

"Start with, when did you leave Glengarry? I don't recollect seeing you there last year. In fact, the only one of our former slaves that I recollect seeing at all was Old Tobias, and I saw him in Hallettsville."

"You didn't see Josephine?"

"I don't think so. Leastways, I don't recall seeing her when I was there. But never mind that. Tell me about you and your family. Where'd they go? Gabriel and Sheba? Where'd they go? And your mammy and her man and the rest of their children? I don't recall seeing any of them when I was there last year."

"They left as soon as the Yankee soldiers come in the spring. Mammy said we was free and we didn't have to live there no more. We could go where we wanted to go, and nobody could tell us that we couldn't. Mammy and Matthew packed up everybody except me, and they set off for Kansas because she said that was a free state before the war and they was sure to be treated good up there."

"So you stayed behind. Why?"

Hannah peered quizzically at Creed, wondering why he should ask such a question. Don't he know? she wondered. Didn't Miss Malinda tell him? She studied him harder. No, he don't know, she finally decided. "I stayed for Dent," she said simply.

Creed's brow narrowed as he asked, "For Dent? Did he make you stay?"

"No, I stayed because I wanted to stay . . . with him."

A wave of memory washed over Creed.

Dent was sitting down, his back against a tree, when Slater returned. He didn't look good; his color was bad, pale.

"How are you feeling, Dent?" asked Slater.

"I've felt better, Clete. Right now, I'm feeling a little puny. You know, like a sick puppy."

Slater knelt down beside his brother and said, "I'd better

take a look at that wound." He loosened the red neckerchief wrapped around Dent's neck, then peeled back the makeshift bandage. Both cloths were heavy with blood. The wound was still bleeding, but that wasn't the worst of it. Slater wiped away as much blood as he could in order to determine the extent of the injury, and that was when he saw that Dent's carotid artery had been nicked badly and that it was bleeding in spurts. Oh, God, no! he thought. Then he hoped that his fear hadn't shown on his face. "We'd better get you to a doctor," he said as calmly as he could.

Dent saw the look in his brother's eyes, and it scared him. He lurched forward, clutched Slater's arm, and said anxiously, "Is it that bad, Clete? Tell me true. Is it that bad?" His voice was filled with the same fright with which he would often awaken when he'd had a childhood nightmare.

And like those times when they were youngsters sharing the same bed, Slater soothed his brother's fears. He patted Dent's hand and said, "No, it's not bad. It's just a nick. It's just that it's best that a doctor look at it as soon as possible. That's all. You'll be fine."

Slater was lying. He'd seen men bleed to death before. It didn't take long. A few minutes sometimes. An hour or two at others. He could only guess at how long Dent had to live.

Dent relaxed and leaned back against the tree again.

"Now you just sit there and take it easy," said Slater, "while I put a clean bandage on you." He removed his own bandanna, folded it, and applied it to the wound. "Hold that in place, Little Breeches, while I tie it up again."

"Little Breeches?" queried Dent. "No one's called me that for years." He thought about it for a second, then added, "Well, at least not since Grandpa Hawk went away. God, I miss him, Clete."

"Me, too," said Slater.

"Did you get all the rustlers?" asked Dent.

"We got most of them," said Slater as he finished tying up Flewellyn's neckerchief around Dent's neck. "Jake is making a count right now."

Some of the men gathered around the two brothers, but none of them spoke. Being war veterans, they knew when a man was dying, and they knew how to show him the proper respect. This was a different case, however. To them, Dent Slater wasn't much more than a boy, and he was their good friend's brother. They were hardened to death on the battlefield; it was a part of war. But this? They weren't sure how to take it.

"Did you find Jess?" asked Dent.

"Yes, I did," said Slater evenly.

Dent swallowed hard and said, "Is he all right?"

Slater started to answer truthfully, but he couldn't. Not now, he couldn't. "Yes, he's fine. He got lost in the dark and wandered around most of the time until I found him this morning. I took him into Orange for a hot meal. I left him there. I told him to catch up to us tomorrow. I came on because the ferryman told me about a bunch of Texas cowboys coming this way a few days back. That's how I figured you boys were in trouble."

"We sure were," said Dent. "I'm glad you're back, Clete. Did you find the Detchens?"

"Not yet. Like I said, Jake is making a head count now." Slater looked up at Pick Arnold. "Go see what's keeping Jake, will you, Pick?"

"Sure thing, Clete," said Arnold, glad to be excused.

"Clete, I'm feeling mighty weak," said Dent. "Are you sure I'm going to be all right?"

"I'm as sure as the sun's going to come up in the east tomorrow morning," lied Slater.

Dent didn't believe him, but he stubbornly refused to let

on that he knew his brother was lying to him, saying, "Clete, I didn't want Glengarry. Not without you."

"I know," said Slater. Suddenly, he realized that Dent knew he was dying, and he felt an indescribable pain in his chest as his heart was rended desolate with grief. He strained mentally to hold back the tears welling up in his eyes but failed.

A faraway gaze came over Dent's eyes as he looked past Slater to a place the living can't see until their time to go there has come. He said, "Clete, I'm starting to feel a little light between the ears. Is that how it's supposed to be?"

"It's all right, Little Breeches," said Slater.

"I'm so tired, Clete, but I want you to know that I didn't want Glengarry without you. I didn't."

All Slater could say was, "I know."

Dent smiled wanly at Slater but only for a second before he said, "Tell Hannah I'll be waiting for her up yonder. Tell her for me, Clete. She's got to know. I love her, Clete. Hannah's my—" Before he could finish, his eyes rolled up, then became glazed. His eyelids fell into a half-closed position, and his lungs wheezed a death sigh.

Oh, God, no! No! Please, God, no!

Slater felt no shame or embarrassment as he took Dent in his arms and wept uncontrollably.

Tears welled in Creed's eyes as he said, "You're Dent's Hannah, aren't you? All this time I thought . . ."

"That his Hannah was some white girl?" said Hannah, finishing the sentence for him as she stood up and went to the chest of drawers.

Creed's head drooped with shame as he said, "Yes." He looked up at her and added, "Did you know that his last words were about you?"

Hannah took her turn remembering.

• • •

Malinda took Clete's letter down back to share it with Hannah. She entered the little one-room house to find Josephine sitting on the edge of the bed, trying to comfort Hannah, who had her face buried in a pillow and was crying softly now.

"I can't get her to stop, Miss Malinda."

"It's all right, Josephine," said Malinda. "You go on now. Go back to your house. I'll take care of her now."

Josephine hesitated. She looked down at Hannah, stroked the girl's hair, then slowly stood up. "Okay, Miss Malinda," she said sternly. "I'll be going, but if you needs me, you just hollers now. You understand, chil'?"

Malinda had become unaccustomed to being mammied by Josephine, but hearing the old woman call her "chil'" again was comforting. To show her gratitude for the support, she hugged Josephine and said, "Thank you, Mammy Joe."

"Don't be thanking me, Miss Malinda. You's the one staying up all night. Not me." And with that, she was gone.

Hannah continued to cry into her pillow, ignoring the changing of the guard.

Malinda sat down on the edge of the bed in the exact spot that Josephine had just vacated. She stroked Hannah's arm tenderly and said, "Hannah, it's Malinda. I came down here to read this letter to you. It's from my brother Clete. He mentions you in it." When the servant made no sign that she was listening to her, Malinda squeezed Hannah's shoulder and added, "I can't say that I understand the pain you're going through now, Hannah, because I'm not feeling the same thing. To tell you something like that would be dishonest, and I can't do that. We've known each other too long to be dishonest with each other now. I hope you're listening to what I'm saying, Hannah. It's important to me and . . . to Dent that you hear what I'm going to read to you now."

Hannah rolled over and looked up at Malinda. Her eyes

were red and raw. She sniffed, then wiped her cheeks with the back of her hand. "Important to Dent?" she queried.

"Yes, Hannah. Just listen and you'll know what I mean." Malinda held up the letter and began to read it aloud:

Dear Malinda,

By now you know that our baby brother has been killed by rustlers in Louisiana. He took a bullet in the neck that cut the big blood vessel that goes up in the head. It was not much of a wound except for this. There was little that we could do to help him as the blood slowly drained out of him. He died peacefully.

We took his body back to Orange where I found an undertaker to take it back to Hallettsville. I wrote to your colonel and asked him to see to it that Dent gets a proper funeral. I know he will honor my request. I wish I could be there with you, but I have my duty to get the herd to market in New Orleans. I hope you understand.

Over these last days of his life, Dent and I had the chance to be brothers once more. We talked a bit about Glengarry. He said that he never wanted it without me. I never doubted that for a minute, not even before this happened. While we were talking, I came to realize that I hardly knew Dent. He was so changed from the boy that I knew as my brother when I left for the war, but never mind all that. I was beginning to like him and respect him as a man. He quit drinking after a few days on the drive as an example to the men. I know it was hard on him in the beginning, but he stuck it out. He did not even ask for a drink after he figured out he was dying.

Like I already wrote, I hardly knew Dent. That is, I hardly knew anything about him. I write this because of the last few minutes of his life and the things he said then.

He was propped up against a tree, and we were talking. He said he did not want Glengarry without me, and I said that I understood what he meant by that. Then he said something that I do not understand because I did not know Dent as well as I wish that I had known him. His final words were about a girl named Hannah. I do not know who this Hannah is, but she must have meant a powerful lot to Dent because of how he said her name. If you know this Hannah, I think it would only be right if you would read this letter to her and let her know that Dent's last mortal thoughts were about her. I hope I am recollecting this correctly as his last words were these. "Tell Hannah I will be waiting for her up yonder. I love her." I think he was about to say that Hannah was his sweetheart, but the Lord took him before he could finish what he wanted to say.

As I wrote already, I do not know who this Hannah is, but I would like to meet her when I return from New Orleans. I think Dent would want me to visit with her for him.

Well, that is all that I have to write for now. I am all right and in good health. I will finish driving the herd to New Orleans, and then I will be home.

Your loving brother,
Clete

Hannah was staring at the letter in Malinda's hand as if it were a precious jewel that had hypnotized her.

"Would you like to keep this letter, Hannah?"

Without shifting her view, Hannah said, "Yes, Miss Malinda." She reached out for it, and Malinda handed it to her. "Thank you, Miss Malinda." She held the letter against her breast and curled up again, but no tears came from her eyes.

"Are you all right now?" asked Malinda.

Hannah smiled. It was a real smile. Natural, not forced. She stared into the distance and said, "I'm just fine now, Miss Malinda. I'm just fine now." In her mind, she added, I am now that I know my Dent will be waiting for me up yonder when my time comes. She rubbed her belly. It's okay, though. I still got part of him down here.

Malinda patted Hannah's arm and said, "You get some sleep now. We'll talk about this some more in the morning." She stood up and left Hannah alone.

Tears trickled down Hannah's cheeks as she opened the top drawer of the chest and took an envelope from it. She handed it to Creed and said, "Yes, Clete, I know about Dent's last words."

Creed opened the envelope and removed the letter inside. He unfolded the pages and recognized it immediately as the one that he'd sent to his sister Malinda the year before when he was in Orange making the arrangements to have his brother's body returned to Hallettsville. He folded the papers and replaced the letter in the envelope. "Did Malinda give this to you?" he asked as he handed it back to Hannah.

"Yes, she did . . . on the night before I stole a horse and left Glengarry for good. I went north to find Mammy and Matthew and the rest of my family in Kansas, but I didn't find them." She snickered and added, "I couldn't even find Kansas."

"So how did you wind up here in Denver?"

"I rode north like I said, riding at night and hiding by day until I come to Nacogdoches. It was there that I met up with some other Negroes heading north. They said that slavery was still legal in the Indian nations and that we should stay away from there. They was gonna go through Arkansas to Missouri and then to Nebraska. I asked them if that was anywhere near Kansas, and they said Kansas was right next door to Nebraska. So I went with them, and we come to a place called Nebraska City where there was some other Negroes living on a farm. I was getting pretty big by then, so they took me in till my time come."

"I don't understand," said Creed.

"My time," she said again. "My birthing time."

"Your birthing time?"

"I'll show you." She stood up, went to the door, slid the bolt back, opened it, then turned back to Creed. "You wait here, Clete. I'll be back in a minute. Don't let nobody come in here while I'm gone."

In the few minutes that Hannah was gone, Creed contemplated everything that she had told him. She was sleeping with Dent, he thought, and evidently it meant more to both of them than anybody else knew. He looked at the cradle, and it struck him what "birthing time" meant. A myriad of thoughts collided with each other in his head, then exploded in a kaleidoscope of emotions. Uncertainly, he reached out and touched the baby bed. Visions of his infant brother lying in another tiny bed flashed before his mind's eye. He tried to focus on the face but couldn't.

The door opened again, and Hannah entered the room holding a sleeping baby wrapped in a small blue woolen blanket. She held it against her breast with her left arm. She closed the door behind her and bolted it again.

Creed took his hand away from the cradle and stood up as Hannah turned to face him.

She lowered the child into the crook of her arm and spread the blanket away from the babe's face. "I named him for his father," she said, gazing proudly at the baby.

"His father?" muttered Creed.

"Cletus McConnell Slater," she said without taking her eyes from the child, "meet your nephew, Warren Denton Slater the Third."

Unsure of what to think, Creed stammered, "You named him . . . for Dent?"

"Uh-huh." She looked at Creed and saw the confusion and anger in his features.

"You can't do that," he blurted. "That baby's not Dent's child."

"Yes, he is," rejoined Hannah.

"No, not legally he isn't. You can't name a Negro bastard for a white man."

Without thinking, Hannah lashed out with her free hand and slapped Creed across the mouth. "Little Dent ain't no bastard, Clete. Dent and me was married all right and proper in the sight of God."

Creed touched his cheek where she had struck him, wondering why he didn't return the blow, but muttering, "Married? That's not possible. You're a . . ." He let his voice drift off.

Hannah finished the sentence for him. "A nigger? Is that what I am to you, *Massuh* Clete?"

Creed shook his head defensively and said, "No, of course not, Hannah."

"Then what am I, Clete? What am I to you? And how about Little Dent? What is he to you?" When Creed didn't answer immediately, she continued the verbal assault. "Look at him, Clete. Look at this beautiful child, and you tell me he ain't your flesh and blood. Look at him, and tell me he ain't your dead brother's son. Go on look at him."

The babe awoke crying.

Creed stared at the bawling child and saw Slater eyes, Slater hair, the Slater jaw, and Slater skin color. "Dent's baby?" he muttered.

"Dent's nigger baby, don't you mean, *Massuh* Clete?"

He didn't know what to say, what to do, except run, get away from this place, from this girl, from this child. He fumbled with the bolt, threw it back, opened the door, and burst from the room.

"Go ahead, Clete," said Hannah after him. "You can run away from us, but that don't change nothing." She sat down on the bed, and her mother's voice echoed in her head.

Dinah Slater knew Hannah's reason for remaining at Glengarry Plantation instead of going with her family to Kansas. She didn't like it, but she understood because she had felt the same about her white lover when she was Hannah's age. "Hannah," she said, "you is a growed up woman now. You can makes your own decisions. If your heart tell you to stay here, then you stays. But you hear me now, girl. You may thinks everything gonna be all right just 'cause your daddy was a white man and my daddy was a white man, but I knows different. You always gonna be a nigger to white folks, and your chillun gonna be niggers, too, no matter if their daddy is a white man, too. Don't make no difference to white folks that you is three parts white and one part black. To them you might as well be all black. That's the way they sees you, Hannah. I know the census man say we is mulattoes, but that don't make no difference. Like I say before, white folks still say we is just niggers. You just keep that in your mind every time you is laying with him."

Hannah felt certain then that her mother was wrong. Dent Slater loved her and had proved his love for her. How, when, and where he had done this was their secret. Until now that she had told Creed that she and Dent had been married in the sight of God.

7

Dan Cooley, a burly six-foot Irishman, walked his police beat like he did every Saturday night, putting in an appearance in every saloon in West Denver once an hour just to let everybody—the good as well as the evil—know that the law was never far away. As he strolled along Fourth Street for the third time since coming on duty, he saw Jimmy Stockton come from the Chicago followed by his shotgun-toting brother Bob. "Now what would that be about?" he asked aloud of no one in particular, but he made up his mind right then and there to find out. He approached the Stocktons as they argued on the boardwalk in front of the saloon.

"You're not going back in there, Jimmy. Not until the Texans are gone."

"But he hit me, Bob," whined the younger brother. "I gotta settle the score with him."

"If you go after that man, he'll kill you for certain."

"Not if he don't see me coming."

Neither of them saw the uniformed policeman striding toward them. "What's this all about now?" demanded Cooley when he stepped up to the brothers. Seeing fear in Jimmy's face, he turned to the older brother and repeated the question. "What's going on here, Bob?"

"It's nothing, Cooley," said Bob.

"The hell it ain't!" argued Jimmy, suddenly bold and hoping to gain an ally in this minion of the law. "There's a Texan in there with a gun—"

"Shut up, Jimmy!" snapped Bob.

"—and he picked a fight with me, Cooley. He kicked me in the balls, then he threatened to kill me with his gun. He put the barrel right up against my nose and—"

"What's this?" interjected Cooley. "Kicked you in the balls and put a gun to your nose?" He looked to the older brother for confirmation again. "Is this true, Bob?"

"Some of it, Cooley," said Bob. "Jimmy's the one who picked the fight, and the Texan finished it for him."

"He was bothering Juanita," said Jimmy.

"That was none of your affair," said Bob.

"Wait a minute," said Cooley. "Does this Texan have a gun on him or not?"

"Yes, he's got a gun," said Jimmy.

"And from what I saw," said Bob, "he knows how to handle it, too."

"And you say he pulled this gun on Jimmy?"

"Jimmy asked for it, Cooley. He started the trouble, and the Texan made him wish he hadn't."

"You say he's a Texan, Bob?"

"Yes, he is," said Bob, "and he was with a couple of other Texans at the bar."

"That's right, Cooley," said Jimmy eagerly. Knowing that the local constabulary harbored a deep prejudice against former slaves, he added, "One of those Texans is a nigger."

Incensed by this fact, Cooley asked, "How come Morton's letting a nigger drink at the bar with white men?"

"That's Morton's business," said Bob.

"It ain't right, Cooley," said Jimmy.

"It's also against the law," said the policeman. "I think I'd better do something about this." He took a firm grip on his nightstick, opened the saloon door, and stepped inside.

"This oughta be good," said Jimmy eagerly.

"You stay here," said Bob, barring his sibling's path with the shotgun. "You hear me, little brother?"

"Aw, come on, Bob. I want to watch Cooley roust the nigger."

"Stay here," said Bob, lowering the weapon and wagging a finger in his brother's face. Seeing that Jimmy would obey the order, although with great reluctance, he followed Cooley into the Chicago, unintentionally leaving the door ajar behind him.

Jimmy peeked into the saloon through the crack in the door and watched Cooley and his brother wade through the crowd that paid them little heed as they moved toward the two Texans still standing at the bar.

Ikard and Brooks envied Creed when he went upstairs with Hannah, and they pitied themselves for not having the courage to approach any of the other women. As consolation, they drank; Brooks continued downing shots of Old Taos, while Ikard finished his first beer and nursed a second. Neither of them noticed the presence of Cooley in the saloon until he tapped Ikard on the shoulder with his billy.

"What do you think you're doing in here, nigger?"

Ikard turned around and saw the uniform before he saw the man. He blinked hard and said nervously, "Just drinking a beer, sir."

The whiskey had done its job on Brooks. He was slow to respond to Cooley's interruption, turning around well after Ikard had answered the policeman. "What's that, Bose?" he asked absently, slurring his words with thick lips and fuzzy tongue.

"Just drinking a beer, you say?" said Cooley.

"Yes, sir."

"What's wrong here?" said Brooks, noting Cooley's dark

blue suit, cavalry style hat, and the shiny badge on his chest.

The noise level in the saloon dropped dramatically as Stockton stepped up behind Cooley.

"Are you with this nigger?" asked the policeman.

Brooks might have been drunk, but he still had his wits about him. "What nigger?" he said with exaggerated indignation as he facetiously looked right through Ikard and surveyed the saloon for the alleged interloper.

Cooley poked Brooks in the chest with his nightstick, pushing the Texan against the bar as he said, "Wise-ass, eh? You'll be speaking to me with respect, bucko, or you'll be spending the night in the city jail."

"I meant no disrespect, sir," said Brooks. "I was only trying to see the nigger you mentioned."

The policeman frowned at Brooks as he perused the Texan's face for any sign of guile. Seeing none, he said, "Don't you know it's against the law for niggers to drink with white men?"

"No, I didn't," said Brooks. "How about you, Bose? Did you know it was against the law for niggers to drink with white men?"

Ikard was wise enough to keep his mouth shut.

Cooley jabbed Brooks in the gut with his billy, forcing the air from the unsuspecting drover's lungs. As the Texan doubled up in pain, the lawman cracked him across the shoulder blades with the club, driving him to the floor and knocking his hat from his head.

Young Stockton stood in the doorway, watching and giggling with delight at the Texans' plight.

When Brooks didn't rise immediately, Cooley said, "You're under arrest for public intoxication, bucko." He looked at Ikard. "As for you, nigger, you'll be moving along or I'll be giving you some of the same."

"Yes, sir," said Ikard. He stooped down to help Brooks,

but Cooley stopped him with a firm touch of the billy on his shoulder.

Creed came down the stairs, his mind aflutter with Hannah's disclosure about her child. He planned to exit the drinking hole without telling Ikard and Brooks, but the unusual quiet of the saloon broke into his thoughts, alerting his senses to danger.

"Just leave him be, nigger. He's under arrest, and I'll be seeing to it that he gets to the jail."

Creed stopped on the next-to-last step as the scene unfolding at the bar attracted his attention.

Ikard looked up at the policeman and said, "But he's hurt, Mr. Lawman."

"I said to leave him be, nigger," said Cooley as he raised his nightstick over his head to strike Ikard.

Creed didn't wait for explanations. A friend needed his aid, and he needed it now. He drew his Colt's and shouted, "Hold it right there, mister!"

The clicking of the hammer on Creed's Colt's rendered the onlooking crowd still with fear in one second and scattering for cover in the next. He aimed the revolver at Cooley's raised arm.

Cooley stayed the blow to Ikard's head. Slowly, he looked over his shoulder at Creed. "Is that the one with the gun?" he asked softly, nervously, so that only Stockton heard him.

"Yep."

Cold sweat beaded on Cooley's forehead and palms, making the nightstick feel greasy in his hand. He lowered the club slowly, and just as cautiously, he turned around to face Creed.

Young Stockton shifted to get a better view of Creed. That sonofabitch! he swore to himself. I'd like to fix him for what he did to me.

Having been to cities like New Orleans and Nashville, Creed recognized the uniform of a policeman, and he reacted by bringing the Colt's to an upright firing position and easing the hammer back to safety. Seeing that control of the situation rested with him, he took the initiative with Cooley. "What seems to be the problem, officer?"

"Problem?" muttered Cooley. Hearing his own voice and realizing how puny it sounded, he cleared his throat and said, "The problem is you and that gun, mister. The law in Denver forbids the carrying of sidearms in public."

"The law in a lot of places forbids the carrying of sidearms in public," said Creed evenly, "but some men still do it."

"Not in Denver, they don't," argued Cooley, feeling bolder by the second. "So I'll be asking you to hand over that pistol and come along peaceful with me to the jail. You're under arrest."

"No, sir, I don't think so," said Creed.

"What?" blustered Cooley. "I said you're under arrest and—"

The policeman's attitude infuriated Creed. "I said no," he insisted. He cocked the Colt's again and leveled it at Cooley's forehead. "I don't know how long you've been in this country, officer, but let me tell you something about America that I learned in school. Our forefathers, the men who made this country, had the good sense to give every man certain rights under the law, and one of those rights is the right to life and liberty. Another one is the right to bear arms to defend ourselves from those people who would take those other rights away from us. Just like you're doing right now, officer. You're trying to take away my gun and my freedom, and I can't let you do that."

"But our law in Denver—"

"To hell with your law in Denver!" snapped Creed. "It's the law of the whole country that comes before any damn law in this city."

Ikard helped Brooks to his feet behind Cooley and Stockton. Brooks was drunk and dazed, but he wasn't totally without his senses. Coming erect, he smiled up at Creed and said, "You tell 'em, Slate."

"Bose, get him out of here," said Creed.

"Yes, sir, Mr. Slate." Ikard bent over and picked up Brooks's hat. They started for the exit, but they hadn't gone far when the door to the gaming room opened and Billy Morton emerged, drawing their attention.

"What the hell is going on, Stockton?" demanded the saloonkeeper. He scanned the room and saw Creed on the stairs. "Not you again. What's the problem now, friend?"

"It's your local policeman, Mr. Morton," said Creed. "He thinks I should hand over my gun and let him lead me off to jail."

"What's this man done, Cooley?" asked Morton.

"He's carrying a gun, and that's against the law in Denver. You know that, Mr. Morton."

"If you arrest him for carrying a gun," said the saloonkeeper, "you'll have to arrest half the men in this place, won't you?"

Cooley thought about that for a second and replied, "There ain't none of them flashing their sidearms at good law-abiding citizens like this here Texan is doing."

"I wouldn't be flashing it if you'd leave my friends be," said Creed.

"That nigger was drinking at the bar with white men," argued Cooley. "That's against the law here in Denver."

"That law don't apply in here," said Morton. "If those Texans want to drink with niggers, that's their business. There's nobody making anybody else drink with them if they don't want. So what's your beef, Cooley?"

"The nigger got uppity with me," said the policeman.

"No, sir, that ain't true," said Ikard in his own defense. "I didn't get uppity with nobody, Mr. Slate."

"Are you calling me a liar, nigger?" spat Cooley.

"No, sir," said Ikard. "I's just saying that you is mistaken. That's all, sir."

"I believe Bose," said Creed. "I've never known him to lie to anybody."

"There you have it, Cooley," said Morton. "Now get out of here, and leave my customers be."

"That's all right, Mr. Morton," said Creed. He eased the Colt's into an upright position, but he didn't uncock it. "We were just leaving anyway." He took the last step to the main floor and moved carefully toward the exit, edging sideways and keeping a cautious eye on Stockton and his shotgun. "Come on, boys. Let's be going."

Ikard and Brooks resumed crossing the room toward the door. Brooks shuffled along, while Ikard warily watched over his shoulder for signs of trouble from the policeman or the guard. They reached the doorway at the same time that Creed did, the three of them lined up like dominoes.

Jimmy Stockton recognized his opening. He flung the door open, slamming it against Brooks who ricocheted like a rubber ball hitting a brick wall, colliding with Ikard who stumbled backward into Creed who lunged forward awkwardly, bumping into a man in a chair and falling over him face first onto a table. Young Stockton compounded his assault by leaping over the sprawled Brooks and Ikard onto Creed's back, collapsing the table beneath them and causing the prone Texan to unintentionally squeeze the trigger of his Colt's and fire off a round.

As if Stockton's sudden attack hadn't been enough to startle every man and woman in the place, the explosion of the revolver scared them all into scurrying for cover.

"What the hell!" mumbled Brooks.

A woman screamed upstairs.

"Kick me in the balls, you sonofabitch!" screeched Stockton as he sat atop Creed. "I'll teach you a thing or two about kicking a man in the balls." He raised his fist and slammed it down on Creed's back, landing the blow between his shoulder blades.

Ikard reacted before anybody. He scrambled to his feet and grabbed Stockton by the wrist when he raised his fist to strike Creed again. Without taking a second to think about it, he wrenched Stockton's arm backward.

POP!

The sickening report of a joint separating sent a wave of horror down the spines of those few who recognized the sound, and Stockton screamed with the instant pain as he toppled from Creed onto his own back on the floor. He held his right shoulder as he cried and writhed in agony on the rough planks.

Ikard bent down to help Creed.

Cooley jerked erect and made a quick surmise of the situation. "The nigger's killed Jimmy Stockton!" he announced to the crowd.

Bob Stockton heard the policeman's pronouncement, but he didn't believe it. He saw clearly that his brother was only hurt, not dying.

"Let's get the nigger!" yelled somebody.

Pandemonium!

Struggling to regain his breath, Creed heard the call for blood, but he felt powerless to do anything about it.

Ikard tried to help Creed to his feet, but he couldn't as several men tore him away from his fallen friend. He fought them with fists and feet, but the effort availed him nothing.

Brooks was helpless as other men took hold of him.

More men wrested Creed's revolver from him and lifted him to his feet unceremoniously.

Morton pulled Stockton's six-shooter, cocked it, and fired a round into the floor to get everybody's attention. When quiet was restored, he said loudly, "Let those men alone." When he wasn't obeyed instantly, he cocked the pistol again and aimed it at the men who held Creed. "Didn't you boys hear me right the first time?"

They released Creed.

"That's better," said Morton. Hearing Jimmy moaning and groaning, he added, "Stockton, see to your brother."

"I'm arresting that man for discharging a firearm within the city limits," said Cooley.

"Calm down, Cooley," said Morton. "None of this would have happened if you'd have let things alone in the first place." He looked back at Creed. "You and your friends had better get going, friend. You've worn out your welcome here."

Creed took his Colt's away from the man who'd taken it from him. "Help me with Tom, Bose," he said. The two of them helped Brooks to his feet, and they headed for the door. Just before exiting, Creed glanced back at the stairs and saw Hannah standing at the top landing holding Little Dent in her arms. He still didn't know what to think about that situation.

Hannah didn't know what to think about Creed either as she watched him and Ikard help Brooks through the saloon door. All she knew for certain was that Little Dent was her son and Creed was her son's uncle—by blood.

8

As eager as he was to get away by himself to mull over Hannah's revelation about her life with Dent and the repercussions that might involve him, Creed felt a stronger responsibility toward Brooks and Ikard. Brooks was too drunk to defend himself, and Creed sensed that Ikard was at great risk in Denver simply because he was a Negro. They needed him now; his other problems could wait.

After depositing Brooks in his room at the California House, Creed led Ikard to their own hotel where they found Loving and Fowler in the dining room eating with a young stranger. Loving waved them over to their table where he introduced them to their dirty, ragged companion.

"This is Billy Taylor, boys," said Loving. After Taylor shook hands with Creed and Ikard, Loving added, "We met Billy on the street today. He's from down your way, Clete. DeWitt County, right, Billy?"

"Yes, sir," said the fuzzy-cheeked teenager eagerly. His blue eyes glistened with excitement as he addressed Creed. "Just across the line from Sweet Home, Mr. Slater."

"I know Sweet Home," said Creed. "It's in the western part of Lavaca County." He and Ikard sat down at the table. "So what are you doing so far away from home, Billy?"

"I came up here looking for my pap. He left Ma and the rest of us kids back in '59 to come up here to prospect for gold. We heard from him kinda regular at the start, but after the war started, we didn't hear nothing no more. So I set out last spring to find him, and I came here."

"I take it you haven't had any luck finding him yet," said Creed.

"No, sir, I haven't found him yet, but I did learn that he moved on to a place called Virginia City up in Montana Territory back in '63. I guess there was another gold rush up there back then."

"Montana," mumbled Creed. "Whew! This country keeps getting bigger and bigger, doesn't it, Oliver?"

"Sure does," said Loving. "Montana. Sounds like a big country. You say it's north of here, Billy?"

"That's what they told me up in Central City. The man said it was way up north, almost all the way to Canada, wherever that is."

"I know where Canada is," said Creed.

"Really?" queried Loving. "Have you been there?"

"No, but I had a chance to go there once."

"When was that, Clete?" asked Loving.

"During the war."

Creed's mind drifted to the recollection of that time back in '64. He was being asked to lead an expedition to Canada that would then invade New England and raise as much hell as possible with the populace before being caught or killed or making an escape back to Canada. The generals showed him a map of the land north of the United States, and they spoke in eloquent terms of doing a great deed for the Confederacy, of striking a blow for freedom, of helping to bring the war to an end with a Confederate victory. All their rhetoric was wasted on him. He declined the offer because he felt they were asking him to make war on civilians and he was vehemently opposed to such treachery.

In his stead, Lieutenant Bennett H. Young accepted the assignment and led the raid on the banks of St. Albans, Vermont, on October 19, 1864, committing one of the first daylight bank robberies in the history of the United States. To Creed's way of thinking, Young could be excused for the deed because he was acting under orders and it was done as an act of war, but he could never have excused himself for making war on innocent people.

"I didn't go to Canada then," said Creed, "but I think I'd like to see that country now." He glanced at Taylor and added, "I'd like to see this Montana you're talking about, too."

"You would? Would you go there with me, Mr. Slater, and help me look for my pap?"

"Sorry, Billy. Not this trip. I got some matters of my own to take care of first."

Taylor's bright eyes showed their disappointment as did his voice. "Sure, yeah. Well, it don't make any difference anyway, Mr. Slater. I ain't even got a horse or much of anything else."

Creed felt a tinge of guilt for placing his own affairs ahead of the lad's request, and the feeling only compounded the confusion that had already fouled his emotions. As a consolation, he offered, "If you're so down on your luck, maybe you could hook on with Mr. Loving here. He'll be needing somebody to replace me. Do you know anything about herding cows?"

"Sure, I do, but ain't you going back to Texas now?"

"Not right away," said Loving. "We're going back to New Mexico from here where we'll be meeting up with my partner who's bringing another herd up from Texas. Most likely we'll be spending the winter in New Mexico and going home in the spring to get another herd to bring up this way."

"I see," said Taylor.

"Even so, Billy," said Loving, "Clete's got the right idea there. You could work for me until you've earned enough money to go up to Montana to look for your father."

"That might take a whole year," said Taylor.

"That's right, it might," said Creed, "but I'm here to tell you that you can't travel this country without a good horse, a good rifle, and some money."

"Clete should know, Billy," said Loving. "He's been traveling for most of the last year or so."

"More like the last five years, Oliver," said Creed. "Even during the war I had to have a good horse and a good rifle, and sometimes I had to have hard money when we ran out of provisions, which happened a lot. Yessir, Billy. You've got to have a good horse, a good rifle, and some money if you want to ride this land looking for your father. Believe me, Billy, there's nothing out there that comes free."

"Don't I know it, though," said Taylor. "Until you bought me this supper, Mr. Loving, I ain't et nothing since last Sunday when the preacher and his wife took me along to dinner at this lady's house. She sure put out a nice spread for us, and she let me cut up some firewood for her to pay for it, too. That was real nice of her. I ain't no charity case like some in this town. I don't take nothing for nothing. No, sir. Not Billy Taylor."

"All the more reason you might want to hook up with our outfit, son," said Loving.

"Well, I'll tell you, Mr. Loving, it's mighty tempting, but if you don't mind, I'd like to talk it over with the parson tomorrow after preaching and see what he says about it."

"That's just fine with me, Billy. What church is this you're going to?"

"Methodist, sir."

"Well, if you don't mind, I'd like to go along with you to preaching tomorrow. How about you, Clete? Do you feel like keeping that promise to your mother to get yourself to worship as often as you can?"

Creed burped a laugh and said, "When you put it that way, Oliver, how can I say no?"

"Good," said Loving as he slapped Creed on the upper arm. "Bose and Jim can come, too." He dug into a vest pocket and removed a silver dollar. He put it on the table in front of Taylor. "Billy, I'm hiring you to come around here in the morning to show us how to get to this church. This is your pay in advance because I don't think you'll let us down and not show up in the morning."

Taylor's eyes lit up again as he stared at the coin.

"Go on and take it, Billy," said Creed. "Oliver wouldn't be doing this if he didn't trust you."

Taylor picked up the dollar, beamed at Loving, and said, "I'll be here first thing in the morning, Mr. Loving. You can depend on it."

"I am, Billy. Now you go on, and we'll see you in the morning." When the youth stood up, Loving looked him over and said, "On second thought, Billy, why don't you stay here with us tonight? Maybe have a bath and put on some clean clothes for tomorrow."

Taylor drooped again, "I ain't got no other duds except these, Mr. Loving."

"Well, not to worry. I'm sure we can fix you up with something. Bose and Jim are about your size. I'm sure they've got a shirt and a pair of pants between them that they can spare."

"Sure we do, Mr. Loving," said Ikard. "We'll fix you up right nice, Mr. Taylor. Won't we, Jim?"

"Sure thing, Bose."

"Then it's settled," said Loving. He looked at Ikard. "Have you eaten yet, Bose?"

"No, sir."

"Well, just sit tight, and we'll get you something to eat. Jim, you take Billy up to our room and show him where the bath is at. Bose will be along after he's had his supper."

Fowler and Taylor nodded in acknowledgement of the order, and they left the table and went upstairs.

As soon as they were gone, Loving said, "Let's get a waiter over here and get you boys something to eat."

"I'm not all that hungry, Oliver."

"Nonsense, Clete. You need to eat. Besides, I want to hear about what you two have been up to since we split up this afternoon." He snapped his fingers, and a waiter hurried over to the table. "Julius, these two men need menus, and I could use another cup of coffee."

"Yes, sir, Mr. Loving," said the waiter, a former slave who had escaped bondage for the freedom of Kansas Territory before the war. He came to Colorado with the hope of finding a fortune in the ground, only to be disappointed like so many other Negro men who discovered that white storekeepers wouldn't advance them any credit for the necessary supplies and tools for prospecting, leaving them no choice except to work at the most menial tasks for the lowest wages. He glanced at Ikard and added, "Coming right up, Mr. Loving." He left them.

"So tell me about your day, Clete. What did you two do after we split up?"

Creed heaved a sigh, then began the report, telling Loving about visiting the various shops and purchasing the new rifle from Rood's gun shop. He paused in his narration when Julius returned with the coffee pot and the menus. He and Ikard ordered fried chicken, boiled potatoes, green beans, cornbread, and coffee.

"So where'd you go after that?" continued Loving.

"Well, we went looking for the other boys," said Creed, "and we found Tom Brooks in a place called the Chicago

Saloon. We had a drink with him, then we took him back to his hotel to sleep off the whiskey he'd drunk."

Ikard smiled mischieviously and said, "That ain't all of it, Mr. Loving. Mr. Slate is leaving out the best parts. He ain't telling you how he went upstairs with a Mexican girl and how he got in a fight with a fellow who didn't like him socializing with the Mexican gal."

"A fight?"

"There wasn't much to it, Oliver," said Creed, trying to downplay the incident. "Just a little whiskey trouble is all."

"Yeah, but there was that Mexican gal," chortled Ikard.

Creed glared at Ikard for a moment, angry that he would make light of the experience. Mexican gal? he thought. He thinks Hannah is a Mexican girl named Juanita. Just like that young sport in the saloon. Just like everybody else in that place. They all think she's a Mexican. She's a Negress, for God's sake!

"Dammit, Bose!" he snapped without raising his voice. "That's none of your business. You've got no right to tell Oliver anything about that. That's my business, and if I want Oliver to know about it, I'll tell him. Do you understand?"

Ikard was dumbfounded, stunned, hurt.

Loving was shocked. He'd never known Creed to make such a display of anger before. Creed was always so calm and detached from everything. Or so he seemed. Now this.

Creed blinked, and he saw the looks on their faces. "Aw, damn!" he spat, even angrier with himself for his fit of pique. He slammed a fist on the table. "Damn me!" He looked at Ikard, his eyes filling with tears of frustration. "I'm sorry, Bose. I had no right to talk to you like that. It's just . . . that . . ." He sucked in a deep breath, forced it out again, and bit his upper lip.

"What's wrong, Clete?" asked Loving softly. "What's troubling you, son?"

Creed's lip popped back into place as he stared at Loving without speaking.

Julius returned with the coffee pot and poured cups of the black brew for Ikard and Creed.

"Thank you, Julius," said Loving, dismissing the waiter.

"I's sorry, Mr. Slate," said Ikard. "I didn't mean nothing by it."

"No, Bose, you don't need to apologize to me," said Creed. "I know you meant no harm." He turned to Loving. "Look, Oliver. I can't stay here. I need some time to myself. I've got a lot on my mind right now, and I need time to think. You understand, don't you?"

"No, I don't, Clete. Does it have something to do with those men who placed the blame on you for their crime?"

"That's part of it, Oliver, and the rest of it I'd rather not talk about, if you don't mind."

"Certainly, son. Anything you say. But before you go gallivanting off somewhere, why don't you eat your supper and get a good night's sleep?"

Creed considered Loving's advice for a moment. Fearing his voice would crack, he nodded his acceptance of the plan, then he fell into a morbid silence that held fast throughout the meal.

As soon as he finished eating, Ikard excused himself and went upstairs to help Fowler outfit Taylor with some clean clothes.

"Now that we're alone," said Loving, "do you want to talk about what's ailing you, Clete?"

"No," said Creed, shaking his head and refusing to give the older man an honest look. He maintained the quiet space between them as they left the table and walked through the hotel and up the staircase to the second floor. When they parted company in the hall, Loving bade him goodnight, and Creed answered with a cordial nod.

Ikard had entered the room only a minute before Creed joined him. "Got Mr. Taylor a good shirt," he said gingerly, "and Jim give him a good pair of pants. Jim already got him a bath by the time I come along. Mr. Taylor's all set for preaching tomorrow."

Creed made no reply. He continued to be sullen even as he and Ikard prepared to retire for the night. Both stripped down to their longjohns before it occurred to Creed that the room had only one bed and it hadn't been determined who would sleep in it and who would sleep on the floor.

Bose had already made up his mind that he would spread his bedroll on the floor and spend the night there. He was stopped in the middle of doing so.

"No, Bose, you take the bed."

"That ain't right, Mr. Slate. You's the one who ought to have the bed."

"Why, Bose? Because I'm a white man? Or at least because most people think of me as a white man? Is that why you want me to have the bed?"

"Yes, sir."

"That's a damn poor reason to give up a bed, my friend." Creed shook his head and reiterated, "A damn poor reason. No. You take the bed, You deserve it."

"So do you, Mr. Slate. You's the boss on the trail. You's the boss here. You ought to be the one to take the bed in the hotel."

"No, Bose, I'm not the boss here. I'm just another man like you."

"All right, but you's the older man here, and the older man ought to be in charge, and that makes you the boss, and the boss gets the bed."

Creed laughed and said, "I don't think I'm gonna win this argument with you, Bose. Not when you keep throwing logic like that at me. I'll tell you what, Bose. I'll toss you for it."

Ikard frowned and said, "Toss me for it? What's that mean, Mr. Slate?"

Creed dug a silver dollar out of the coin pocket of his trousers and showed it to Ikard. "This dollar has a seated lady on one side and an eagle on the other."

"Who is that lady, Mr. Slate?"

"The school teacher back in Hallettsville called her Lady Liberty."

Ikard beamed and said, "Miz Freedom. Lady Liberty. All the same, Mr. Slate."

"That's right, Bose. It's all the same. No matter whether you call it freedom, liberty, manumission, or emancipation it all means the same thing. It means you're free to make your own decisions, your own choices. And that brings us back to who gets to sleep in the bed. I'm gonna flip this dollar in the air, and while it's in the air, you say lady or eagle. I'll catch the dollar in one hand and put it on the back of the other. Like this." He demonstrated. "If the one you call is showing, then you get the bed and I sleep on the floor. If the one you don't call is showing, I get the bed and you sleep on the floor. Fair enough?"

Ikard nodded and said, "Fair enough."

Creed flipped the dollar in the air.

"Lady," said Ikard.

Creed caught the coin with his right hand and slapped it down on the back of his left. He showed the coin to Ikard and said, "Lady. You get the bed."

"I still don't know about that, Mr. Slate. Somehow it don't seem right for me to be sleeping in the bed and you to be sleeping on the floor."

"Bose, you'd better get used to it. You're a free man now, and you're entitled to all the same rights as me or any other man in this country. No matter what their color or their religion or their politics might be. Do you understand that?"

"Yes, sir, I do, but do all the white folks understands it?"

Creed smiled at Ikard and said, "Good question, Bose." Hell, he thought, I'm not even sure I understand it. Not now anyway. "Yes, Bose, that's a really good question, and I don't have an answer for it."

"I gots one, Mr. Slate," said Ikard in absolute solemnity. "The answer is no. All the white folks ain't never gonna understand that every man is just as free as the next man no matter what his color or his religion or his politics is. Some of them is gonna understand it and live just fine with it, and some of them is gonna not understand it, and they ain't gonna let people who's different from them live free and easy like them. That's the way it's always been in the past, Mr. Slate, and that's the way it's always gonna be in the future."

"Do you really think so, Bose?"

Ikard's lips tightened together as he nodded an affirmation of his words.

"Well, we'll have to do everything we can to change things for the better, won't we?" said Creed.

Ikard smiled again and said, "Yes, sir."

"And we'll start by you taking the bed and me taking the floor because you won that coin toss fair and square."

"Yes, sir."

Creed threw his bedroll on the floor, spread it out, and started to lie down.

Ikard picked up the pillow from the bed and handed it to Creed. "You can least have this pillow, Mr. Slate," he said. "I can use my bedroll for resting my head."

"Thank you, Bose," said Creed, accepting the pillow. He lay down for the night, and Ikard blew out the lamp on the dresser. Looking at the ceiling in the dark, Creed had a thought. "Bose, if your brother married a white woman and they had a child, how would you feel about the child? I mean, if the child was born a white boy."

Ikard was slow to reply, but when he did, he spoke with strength. "I'd love my brother's child no matter if it was born a green boy."

Silence.

9

The next morning Creed wanted to take leave of his fellow Texans as soon as he rose, but Loving wouldn't hear of it, leastways not until they had attended worship. "Don't forget your promise to your mother, Clete," he said gently. Creed couldn't argue with him; he attended the religious services.

Billy Taylor led his newfound friends to the Methodist Episcopal Church at the corner of Lawrence and E Streets. They were met at the front doors by a husky, black-bearded man who recognized young Taylor. "Good morning, Billy," he said with a tobacco-stained smile through his thick whiskers.

"Good morning, Mr. Brown."

"Are these gentlemen with you, Billy?"

Taylor introduced Henry C. Brown to the other Texans, including Ikard and Fowler.

Brown was the carpenter who had loaned a building to the church a few years earlier as a house of worship until the present edifice could be constructed. He acknowledged Creed and Loving with a friendly "How do you do, gentlemen?" After they replied in kind, he turned to the two former slaves and said, "As for you boys, there are two churches for coloreds three blocks over and two blocks up on Holliday Street between H and I Streets. I think you would feel more comfortable hearing God's word in one of them."

"Now hold on there," said Loving.

"No, Mr. Loving," said Ikard. "It's all right. He's right. Jim and me would be more comfortable hearing the Lord's word coming from one of our own."

"Are you certain about that, Bose?" asked Loving.

"Yes, sir."

"All right. Go ahead and go to one of those churches. We'll meet you back at the hotel after worship."

Ikard and Fowler strolled away on their own.

Brown escorted Loving, Creed, and Taylor to a visitors' pew in the rear of the hall where they participated in the singing and listened politely to the sermon delivered by Rev. B. T. Vincent. Seated in the last row, the Texans observed the regular members of the church in front of them. Taylor knew many of the people by name, but they were all strangers to Loving and Creed—with one exception maybe. A young woman that Creed thought he recognized as someone out of his distant past. Creed hoped she would turn so he might get a better view of her, but she remained focused on the preacher throughout the service.

After the rite of communion, the tall, thin, bearded minister concluded the weekly ceremony by asking God's blessing on the congregation. With a final amen, he marched up the aisle to the doors, threw them open, then posted himself outside on the landing where he could receive the congregation.

As the Texans waited patiently for their turn to leave the building, Creed tried to get a better view of the woman with the familiar face. Although the line moved slowly, Creed had no luck spotting the lady. When the Texans finally edged into the line and moved to its head, Taylor shook Vincent's hand vigorously, released it, and said, "Reverend, I'd like you to meet Mr. Oliver Loving and Mr. Slate Creed. They're from Texas like me."

Vincent gave them each a limp handshake and said, "Yes,

gentlemen, I believe I read about you in the newspapers recently. Didn't you bring a herd of cattle to this vicinity this past month and deliver it to Mr. Iliff on his ranch downriver from Denver?"

"That we did, Reverend Vincent," said Loving. "And tomorrow we'll be heading back to New Mexico Territory to meet my partner who should have another herd for us to bring up here in the spring."

"That is wonderful news, Mr. Loving. Colorado has such a scarcity of cattle at this time that the price of beef is truly outrageous."

"So I hear," said Loving. "Well, we'll certainly do our best to alleviate that situation, Reverend. You can count on that much from Texas, sir."

"Reverend Vincent, Mr. Loving has offered me employment as a drover," said Taylor.

Vincent's narrow face darkened paternally as he said, "That's wonderful news, Billy, but does this mean that you'll be giving up your search for your father?"

"That's what I wanted to speak to you about, Reverend. I'm not so sure that I should accept Mr. Loving's offer because it would mean I'd have to put off going to Montana to look for Pap. But on the other hand, I could earn enough money to buy me a decent horse and all the trappings I'd need to make a trip up there to Montana and have a proper look-see for him. Which way do you think I should go, Reverend?"

Vincent appraised Loving with a glance and said, "I think you'd be wise to accept Mr. Loving's offer, Billy."

"That's what we told him, Reverend," said Loving. "Didn't we, Clete?"

Creed made no reply, his attention being elsewhere, his eyes searching for that familiar female face that he thought he'd seen during the service. He was trying to locate the lady who had vanished in the crowd of worshippers now loitering in front of the church.

"Didn't we, Clete?" repeated Loving, nudging Creed with an elbow.

"What, Oliver?" muttered Creed, turning back to Loving. "I'm sorry, I wasn't listening. What did you say?"

"I was just telling the reverend here that we'd told Billy that he'd be better off working for me."

"Yes, that's right, Reverend," said Creed. "I even told him that I'd like to see Montana, and to tell you the truth, if I had the opportunity, I'd be sorely tempted to go with him." And with that, he shifted his gaze back to the milling churchgoers.

Taylor became agitated with excitement. "You'll go with me, Mr. Creed? That'll be great."

Creed didn't hear the lad clearly, his attention once more focused elsewhere.

"I said that'll be great, Mr. Creed," repeated Taylor.

Loving nudged Creed again.

"What's that you say, Billy?" asked Creed.

"I said that'll be great. You going to Montana with me, I mean."

"Hold on, Billy," said Creed, realizing that he'd better focus on the conversation before he got himself into a fix. "I said I'd be sorely tempted to go with you. I didn't say I'd go with you. I've got business of my own to take care of before I can even think about traipsing off to Montana. Besides that, it's too early for you to be making any plans to ride off to Montana. You haven't even earned that horse Mr. Loving promised you as part of your pay."

"Wait a minute, Clete. I didn't say anything about giving Billy a horse."

"But you were going to, weren't you, Oliver?"

Loving frowned. Creed had stuck him in that narrow gap

between a rock and a hard place, and with the parson standing there listening intently, he knew that he had only one way out of it. "Yes, I suppose I was," he said. "Why not? If it would help him find his father, it's the least I can do to help. What's one horse more or less? Right, Reverend Vincent?"

"That's right, Mr. Loving. God bless you, sir, for aiding this good lad. Billy, I think you're in good hands with Mr. Loving and Mr. Creed here."

"Please excuse me, Reverend," said Creed absently, "but I must be going. I think I saw someone that I haven't seen in a long time." Without waiting for the minister to excuse him, he moved off toward a group of women and children gathered at the street corner.

The ladies conversed animatedly with each other, and several youngsters cavorted like spring calves put out to pasture for the first time.

Creed's heart beat faster, and a cold sweat made his palms greasy to the touch as he came close to the lady that he thought might be Mattie Whittaker, the girl that he'd left behind in Kentucky during the war.

Matilda Whittaker had been rather plain looking with curly dishwater-blonde hair. She wore wire-rimmed spectacles that disguised blue eyes that could sparkle like diamonds when she was happy and that could be icy cold when she was angry. With pale skin and a straight-lipped mouth, she was really quite pretty when she smiled, and Creed had been in love with her.

Is it her? Creed asked himself as he approached the knot of women chatting so gaily. What if it is? What do I say after four and a half years? What will she say? His mind flooded with memories: their first meeting at the women's college in Russellville, Kentucky; their first kiss; the one and only time that they made love; Ginny Rapp berating him for leaving

Mattie behind to face the consequences of their lovemaking; her parents screaming at him and threatening his life when he called on them earlier that year; the beating that her brothers had tried to give him for deflowering their sister; and the realization that he had made Mattie pregnant and that she had left Russellville to hide her shame and have his child. He hesitated several feet away from the lady as doubts crossed his mind.

Some of the women ceased speaking in order to admire the handsome Texan approaching them. In their number was the young woman that Creed had thought might be Mattie. She did resemble Mattie in several aspects: hair color the same, eyes blue but lighter in shade, thin and angular, rosy cheeks, but no eyeglasses. She wasn't Mattie, not the Mattie that Creed remembered.

A mixture of disappointment and relief painted Creed's face, much to the surprise of the ladies. Caught by their gazes, Creed blushed with embarrassment, tipped his hat to them, and said, "Ladies."

"Good day, sir," said the young woman that had drawn his attention.

Realizing that he should explain his curiosity or be thought a rude fellow, Creed stepped forward, removed his hat, and said, "Please forgive me, ma'am, but I thought I recognized you as someone I once knew. Now that I see you close up I see that I was mistaken."

"A pity, sir," she said.

"Uh, Creed, ma'am. Slate Creed."

"How do you do, Mr. Creed? I am Mrs. Charles Williams. I own a millinery shop on Larimer Street."

"It's an honor to meet you, Mrs. Williams."

A small girl with long black hair ran up to the lady, tugged at the skirt of the lady's dark green dress, and said, "Time to go, time to go."

"You mustn't interrupt grown-ups when they're talking, darling," said Mrs. Williams. "It's not polite."

"Oh, it's all right," said Creed, smiling at the child. "I don't mind." He knelt down for a better look at the girl. "What's your name?" he asked.

Without fear, she said, "Cletia."

"That's a pretty name. A pretty name for a pretty girl."

And she was. Besides dark tresses that hung to her shoulders, she had amber-flecked green eyes, rosy cheeks, and a naturally golden complexion. "Thank you, sir," she said.

"And you're so polite, too. How old are you, Miss Cletia?"

Cletia held up three fingers and said, "This many."

"Three years old. My, my. And so polite, too." He glanced up at Mrs. Williams, then back at the girl. "Do you want to know a secret, Miss Cletia?"

"Oh, yes," said the child, her head bobbing eagerly.

"Well, I thought this pretty lady—" he nodded at Mrs. Williams "—was a pretty lady that I once knew a long time ago."

"How long ago?" asked Cletia.

"Oh, a long time ago." Seeing that the girl didn't understand the concept of time yet, he thought to put his tale in terms that she could comprehend. "In fact, it was so long ago that the pretty lady was actually a princess and I was a knight with a shiny sword."

Cletia's eyes danced with delight as she shrieked, "Oh, yes, just like in the fairytale."

"Yes, just like in the fairytale. But that was a long time ago, and I'm no longer a knight with a shiny sword, and the princess went off to live in a land far away."

The child's joy turned sour. "The princess didn't live happily ever after?"

Seeing the sadness in Cletia's face, Creed said, "Oh, I'm sure she did."

"But how could she without her knight?"

Creed was caught, and he knew it. Out of the mouths of babes, he thought. "I don't know the answer to that one, Miss Cletia. Maybe the ending to the story hasn't been written yet. Maybe the knight will find her, and they'll live happily ever after. It's hard to say right now." He straightened up and said, "I'm sorry to have bothered you, Mrs. Williams. If you'll pardon me, I must be going now."

"Of course, Mr. Creed."

He bent over to the little girl and said, "It was an honor to meet you, Miss Cletia."

Cletia curtsied and said, "Thank you, sir."

He straightened up again, donned his hat, tipped it to Mrs. Williams, and said, "Good day, ma'am." He turned away to rejoin Loving and Taylor.

"Who was that man, Auntie?" asked Cletia as she watched Creed walk away.

"Just a stranger, Cletia," said Mrs. Williams as she also gazed after Creed. Once he was out of earshot, she took Cletia's hand and said, "Come along now, darling. We'd best be going home before your mother begins to worry about us."

"Yes'm," said Cletia.

The woman and child moved away toward their home on Larimer Street.

Loving, Creed, and Taylor headed off in the opposite direction toward their hotel.

"Was she who you thought she was?" asked Loving.

"No, she was somebody else," said Creed as he tried to hide his disappointment. "A Mrs. Williams."

"I know her," said Taylor. "She's a widow. Her husband was killed in the war. Somewhere in the Indian nations, I heard."

"That figures," said Creed dryly.

"Her cousin from Kentucky lives with her," said Taylor. "She wasn't in church today. I wonder if she's ill again. I'll have to ask Reverend Vincent about her."

"You do that, Billy," said Creed absently. He thought more of Mattie Whittaker, recalling how they'd met and how they'd parted.

When the Confederate army occupied Kentucky in the late summer of 1861, the 8th Texas Cavalry was assigned to patrol an area that covered Logan, Warren, Edmondson, Hart, and Barren counties. Their job was to watch out for any encroachment of Union forces coming south from Louisville with Bowling Green as their strategic goal. The Texas companies were placed under the command of local generals, and to make them more effective, they were paired with Kentucky units.

Creed's outfit, Company F, had the duty of protecting the western reaches of Logan County. During the day, they scouted the two roads that went west out of Russellville to Elkton and to Tightsville over in Todd County; at night, they posted pickets in the outlying areas, while the majority of the men bivouacked west of Russellville near Walnut Grove. At every opportunity afforded them, the troopers rode into town to go "skirt hunting" or drinking. It was during one of these excursions that Creed met Mattie.

Autumn leaves were still falling from the trees when Creed rode into Russellville with a half dozen other Texas boys. They had heard that Russellville Collegiate Institute at Seventh and Summer Streets was attended by some of the prettiest, smartest, and—above all—friendliest girls in Kentucky. They thought they'd have a look for themselves to see if this statement should prove true or false.

The Texans rode up to the school, and from the street, several of them called out to the girls in the dormitory that was built onto the brick classroom building. Giggling and laughing, some of the young ladies opened their windows and leaned out to talk to these gallant young men from far-away Texas. One merely stood at her window, glaring out at the boisterous soldiers. Of the three adjectives that they had heard applied to the Russellville girls, only one appeared to fit her: smart.

"That one's for you, Slater," said Jack Blackburn, pointing to the girl behind the closed window.

"Is that so?" shot back Creed. Then a thought occurred to him. "Tell you what, Blackburn. I'll bet you a dollar that I can get her to smile before you can talk one of those gigglypusses into coming out here to meet you close up."

"Too easy, Slater," said Blackburn. "Make her open her window and talk to you and smile, then you've got a bet."

Creed thought about it for a second, then said, "You've got a bet, Blackburn." And with that, he kicked Nimbus in the ribs, gave out a Texas yell, and charged up the lawn to the building.

The girl's window was on the second floor near the corner of the dormitory, and the rain pipe ran right by it. Creed climbed up on his horse's back, stood on the saddle, then pulled himself up the rain pipe until he was beside the girl's window.

"What are you doing out there?" she shouted through the glass.

Creed held on to the pipe with one hand and cupped his ear with the other, pretending to be unable to hear her. "What?" he shouted back.

"What are you doing out there?" she repeated. "Are you insane?"

Creed continued to feign his inability to understand her. "What's that you say?" he shouted.

Exasperated, she unlatched her window and threw it open.

"I said, what are you doing out there? Are you insane?"

"No, ma'am, I'm not insane," said Creed with as straight a face as he could muster. "If I was, I wouldn't think you're the prettiest thing I've seen yet in this here Kentucky town."

The girl gasped, covered her mouth with her hand, and backed away from the window.

"My name is Clete Slater, ma'am." He tipped his hat with one hand, while maintaining a precarious grip on the rain pipe with the other. He replaced the hat, then said, "I hail from Lavaca County, Texas, ma'am, and I'm in the Confederate army, as you can plainly see by my uniform. Dandy, ain't it?" When she made no reply, he continued, saying, "I was just passing by and—"

Creed was unable to finish the sentence because the rain pipe came loose from the gutter at the top just then. He held on for dear life as the pipe bent away from the wall, leaving him dangling high above the ground.

The girl gasped again and rushed forward to the window. "Oh, sir," she said, "are you all right?"

"Not to worry, ma'am," he said, holding tightly to the pipe. "It's all right. Just watch." He gave out a piercing whistle that his horse recognized as a summons.

The Appaloosa positioned himself beneath him as if he had done this sort of thing on several occasions.

With perfect nonchalance, Creed dropped into the saddle, grabbed the reins, kicked Nimbus into a gallop, and rode off, swinging his hat over his head and screaming like a Comanche. As soon as he reached the street corner, he tugged on the reins, halting the stallion and replacing his hat on his head, then he turned the animal around and raced back to the dormitory. As Nimbus galloped past the building, Creed leapt off the horse but held on to the saddle. When his feet hit the ground, he bounced up and over the horse's back, landing on the other side, and again he bounced up and over the horse's back. He repeated this trick twice more before regaining his posture in the saddle. When horse and rider reached the other street corner, he halted Nimbus again and rode back to accept the applause of all the girls in the dormitory except the one he wanted to smile. Chagrined, he rode up to her window again. He looked up at her blank stare and said, "I must be insane after all, ma'am."

"Why is that?" she asked evenly.

"A sane man wouldn't do what I just did just because he wanted to see a girl smile."

"Is that why you did that? To impress me?"

"Didn't I say you were the prettiest girl in Russellville?"

"That proves you're insane, sir."

"No, ma'am, it only proves the poet's words," said Creed.

Her brow wiggled a bit in curiosity. "The poet's words, sir?" she queried.

"Yes, ma'am. The ones about beauty being in the eyes of the beholder. In my case, my Grandpa Hawk always taught me to see with my heart and not just with my eyes. That's why I say you're the prettiest girl I've seen in this Kentucky town."

A smile came over the girl's lips, and a sparkle danced in her blue eyes. She leaned through the window and said, "Please stop addressing me as ma'am. It makes me feel old. My name is Matilda Whittaker, but I'd rather you called me Mattie."

Creed took another look at Mattie. A more serious view. And he recollected his grandfather Hawk McConnell telling him that everything is not always as it seems on first sight. That old Choctaw warrior was right. Especially in this case. Mattie was really quite pretty when she smiled. Creed felt a flutter in his heart as he removed his hat again and said, "I'm pleased to make your acquaintance, Miss Whittaker."

"No, please," she said, "call me Mattie."

Blackburn rode up and said, "All right, Slater, you win. I owe you a dollar."

Mattie's smile vanished. She frowned at Blackburn.

"No, you don't," said Creed.

"Sure, I do," said Blackburn. "You got this girl to open her window and talk to you, and she smiled. You win the bet."

"What's this all about, Mr. Slater?" demanded Mattie.

"Never mind that now, Jack," said Creed.

"No, sir," said Blackburn. "A bet is a bet, and I am not a man to cheat on a bet."

Now Mattie understood, and she was furious. "You made a wager that you could entice me to open my window and that I would speak with you and I would smile at you?" she gasped. "Well, I never!"

"Yes, it's true," said Creed with all the honesty that his two grandfathers had taught him since childhood, "but that was before you spoke to me, Mattie Whittaker."

"What's this, Slater?" asked Blackburn in mocking disbelief. "Don't tell me you're taken with this homely crone. I ain't believing that, boy."

Creed reached over and grabbed the reins to Blackburn's horse. He gave them a quick jerk that forced the animal off balance, causing it to stumble and fall sideways, throwing Blackburn to the ground.

Blackburn rolled onto his back, propped himself onto one elbow, and said angrily, "What the hell was that for?"

"I believe you owe Miss Whittaker an apology, Jack," said Creed evenly.

Blackburn snickered and said, "The hell, you say. I ain't a-gonna do it. You want to apologize to her, you go right ahead, but I sure as hell don't intend to do it." He started to get up.

Creed leapt from the saddle and landed on Blackburn's back, sprawling him on the ground again. Creed scrambled to gain the upper hand, straddling Blackburn and forcing his face into the grass with one hand while his other put pressure on Blackburn's neck. Blackburn tried to buck Creed off his back, but as soon as he tried this maneuver, he paid for it. Creed grabbed his hair and slammed his face into the ground.

"No, sir," said Creed through clenched teeth. "I said you were to apologize to the lady."

"Mr. Slater, please," pleaded Mattie.

"No, ma'am," said Creed over his shoulder. "He had no call to say that about you, and he's going to apologize for it." He jerked Blackburn's head up and said, "Aren't you, Jack?"

Blackburn gasped for air, and when he caught his breath, he swore, "Goddamn you, Clete Slater! You'll pay for this!"

Without waiting for another word, Creed made a fist and slammed it into Blackburn's spine at the base of his neck. The force of the blow snapped Blackburn's head face-first into the grass, leaving Creed with a handful of greasy hair. Feeling Blackburn's form go limp beneath him, Creed realized that he had knocked him unconscious. To make certain that Blackburn was out cold, Creed turned his head sideways and lifted an eyelid to see if his eyes were rolled up; they were. Creed stood up and looked down at Blackburn, then he remembered Mattie Whittaker. He shifted his view to her.

"I'm really sorry about that, Miss Whittaker," he said. "He had no call to say what he did."

"He isn't dead, is he?" asked Mattie.

The other soldiers rode up now.

"No, he's just got his lamp put out is all," said Creed. "He'll have a good headache tomorrow, but he'll live."

"You best not be around when he comes to," advised Marsh Quade. "He won't soon forget this, Clete."

Creed glared at Quade and said, "Why don't you just shut

up, Marsh, and get Jack on his horse and take him back to camp?"

"What are you going to do, Clete?" asked Quade.

Creed looked up at Mattie and said, "Now that all depends, don't it?"

Quade understood. He dismounted, and with the help of the other soldiers, he placed Blackburn over his saddle and took him back to camp.

Creed stuck around to explain things to Mattie, but she said no explanation was necessary. His actions had said all that she wanted to know. He asked for permission to call on her, and she gave it readily. He said he would be calling soon . . .

Rumors had come down to the troops that with the fall of Fort Henry on the Tennessee River in early February General Albert Sidney Johnston was planning to withdraw all Confederate forces from Kentucky and set up a defensive line from Memphis to Nashville. Creed's unit heard that they were to cover the evacuation of Bowling Green, then ride to the aid of the men that were soon expected to come under siege at Fort Donelson on the Cumberland River.

Like most of the other soldiers who had found sweethearts in the area, Creed mounted up and rode into Russellville for one last kiss and to say good-bye to the girl he was leaving behind. He found Mattie at the college, waiting for him inside the front door.

"We're going to pull out tomorrow," said Creed. "Maybe tonight. I don't know for sure when yet."

"I know," said Mattie softly. "We heard already."

"I came to see you one more time," said Creed. "I wish I didn't have to go. I wish those Yankees would go back north of the Ohio River and leave us alone down here."

"If it wasn't for the war," said Mattie, "we would have never met."

Creed peered at her quizzically and said, "I suppose that's one way of looking at it, but you're the only good thing that's come out of this war so far for me."

"I'm frightened that I'll never see you again, Clete," said Mattie anxiously. "Isn't there any way that you could stay here?"

"No, Mattie, there isn't. I have to go with my company. There's lots of other fellows who want to stay here as badly as I do, but if we all stayed, who would be left to fight the Yankees? No, Mattie, I have to go."

She looked around the foyer at the other couples there. "Come on," she said. "We can't say farewell properly here." She led him through the building to the door to her room. "Wait here while I get my wrap." She left for a brief minute, then returned wearing a long brown cape. Taking his hand, she said, "Come on," and she led him out the back door of the school.

The winter night was cold, crisp, and clear. As Mattie led Creed across the rear yard, the young lovers could see their breath steaming in the air. They crossed the street and walked between two houses to a barn in the rear of one. Mattie scanned the darkness to make certain that they hadn't been seen, then she quietly opened the door and took Creed inside. After closing the door behind them, she took his hand again and led him to the ladder that went up to the loft. They climbed in silence until they reached the hay mow. Mattie found the right spot and pulled Creed down beside her. She lay back, untied the string of her cape, and spread it out on the hay.

"Now, Clete Slater, I want you to give me a proper farewell," she whispered.

At first, Creed was unsure of what she meant, but after a few wet kisses, he knew. He wasn't inexperienced in lovemaking, having had the frivolous pleasure of enjoying the promiscuous May sisters, Lucy and Marcella, more than once each. Both being full of experience, they had taken the time to teach Creed what a woman wanted from a man when she was in the throes of passion. And now Mattie was giving him the opportunity to use that carnal knowledge. They made love several times through the night until the cocks began crowing just before dawn.

"Come on," said Creed. "We have to get back."

"I don't want to go," said Mattie. "I want this night to last forever."

A rooster reminded Creed that daylight was breaking. "I wish it would go on forever, too," he said, "but the world stops for no one. Or so I've heard. We must go, Mattie."

She pulled him to her one more time and said, "Give me one last kiss, then you may go, Clete."

He kissed her long and hard, then broke away. He refused to look back and see the tears streaming down her cheeks. He slipped out of the barn and was soon on the way back to his camp.

"Reverend Vincent invited us to dinner, Clete," said Loving, breaking into Creed's thoughts. "I think I'll go. How about you?"

"I don't think so, Oliver. I've got other plans."

"You ought to come along, Mr. Creed. Mrs. Vincent is a fine cook, and you can meet—"

"I said I have other plans, Billy," snapped Creed. He halted right there on the sidewalk, grabbed Loving's arm, and stopped him as well. "If you don't mind, Oliver, I'll take my leave of you now. I've got a lot on my mind, and I'd like to be alone for a spell. I thought I'd ride Nimbus up into the hills for a while. Maybe a few days. I don't know how long for sure, but I'm not coming back here until I get a few things straight in my mind."

"I wish you'd tell me what's troubling you, son," said Loving, "but I know you won't. So I'll say good-bye to you right here and now. Godspeed, Clete Slater." He offered his hand to Creed.

"Good luck to you, too, Oliver," said Creed as he shook Loving's hand. "Say good-bye to Bose and Jim and the others for me, will you?"

"Sure thing, Clete."

Creed turned to Taylor. "Good-bye, Billy. If you're still wanting to ride to Montana to look for your father the next time we meet, well, maybe I'll just ride along with you. In the meantime, you listen to everything Mr. Loving tells you, and you'll never go wrong."

"I don't understand why you're going, Mr. Creed, but I guess you got your reasons. Good luck to you."

They shook hands, and Creed walked off toward the Elephant Corral to have his horse made ready for traveling.

"Billy, there goes a man who's hurting deep inside his soul, and you know what?"

"No, sir. What?"

"There's not a single thing anybody can do about it. Nobody except him."

10

After checking out of the Colorado House, Creed figured his chances of finding some solitude would be greater out on the plains east of the city than in the hills to the west. He headed off in that direction, thinking that he would sort out his feelings about Hannah and Little Dent and the turmoil caused by seeing Mrs. Williams, who reminded him so much of Mattie Whittaker. Once he had himself straight again, he would return to Denver and begin looking for Marshall Quade.

As he rode along Arapahoe Street, a beautiful woman with raven hair and deep chestnut eyes sitting on the stoop of a two-story brick house caught his eye. "Good afternoon, stranger," she called to him. She wore a low-cut cardinal dress that exposed her cleavage.

"Ma'am." He tipped his hat to the lady as a matter of courtesy, not thinking that the gesture would lead to a delay in his exit from Denver.

"What's your hurry, handsome?" She stood up and put a hand on her right hip. "It's Sunday, don't you know?"

Creed snickered to himself. *I should have known,* he chastised himself. *Only a lewd woman would be so forward.* Suddenly and oddly curious about her, he reined in Nimbus and guided the Appaloosa to the hitching post in front of the house. "So it is," he said with a friendly smile as he doffed his hat.

"You must be new in town."

"What makes you think that?"

"Well, I've never seen you around here before, and I know every handsome man in Denver."

Creed laughed and said, "Yes, I'll bet you do at that."

"The name is Addie LaMont, and this is my house." She indicated the structure behind her with a wave of her hand. "Why don't you climb down and come in for a drink so we can get better acquainted?"

"I can't believe business is so slow, Miss LaMont, that you have to invite men in from the street."

"My business hasn't been slow since the first week I arrived in this town, mister."

Addie LaMont spoke the truth. Her real name was Ada, and she came from a solid Northeastern family. At seventeen, she married Reverend Thomas Sheridan, the young minister of her church. She took pride in fulfilling her duties as a pastor's helpmate, and when the first news of gold echoed across the Plains from the Rockies and the youthful preacher felt called to carry the gospel into the wilderness, Ada gladly accompanied him west.

The couple joined a wagon train at St. Joseph, Missouri, in the summer of '58, and for a week all seemed well. Then Reverend Sheridan disappeared one night. A hasty investigation disclosed that two horses and a young woman of doubtful reputation were also missing. The wagonmaster halted the train for a full day while search parties fanned out from the trail to look for them. It availed them nothing; no trace of the man and woman or the horses could be found. Only one possible assumption could be made: Mr. Sheridan and the woman had run off together, leaving poor Ada to be pitied and comforted by the other immigrants.

During the long, lonely days that followed, Ada maintained a stony silence, finally finding her voice when the wagon train reached Denver. On that day, she stood before her fellow travelers and announced, "You see me for the last time as a God-fearing woman. Tomorrow I start the first brothel in this settlement. In the future, my name will be Addie LaMont. Any of you men in need of a little fun will always find the flaps of my tent open."

Addie's sensational debut into her newly chosen profession was delayed briefly, however. News of her announcement accompanied with descriptions of her striking beauty spread through the area with the speed of a cyclone, going so far as to attract the attention of a friendly band of Arapahoes who decided to visit the wagon train. One young chief was so impressed by the dark-eyed charmer in the red calico dress that he offered to trade five ponies for her. None of the new arrivals were acquainted with the ways of Arapahoe courtship, and Addie, thinking the whole affair a joke, nodded her agreement. The chief returned the next day with several warriors and the five ponies. Addie took a hasty refuge in a covered wagon, while the wagonmaster told the Indians that she had only been joking with him. The chief failed to see the humor in the matter. He argued that a deal was a deal, and if the woman didn't become his wife he would lead his warriors against the white men. The captain of the train called his bluff as a dozen men backed him with rifles and shotguns, and the Arapahoe gave up and went home disappointed.

Once her Indian problem was solved Addie kept her word to the men of Denver. Within a week, she was open for business in a cabin located in Auraria's Indian Row on the banks of the South Platte. As the settlement prospered, so did she. Within a year, she left her shack on Indian Row and moved into the two-story house where Creed met her in 1866.

"What did you say your name was?" asked Addie.

"I didn't, but if you must know, it's Creed. Slate Creed from Lavaca County, Texas."

"From Texas, you say? Well, welcome to Denver, Mr. Creed. We don't get many Texans here these days. Not since before the war. Did have one earlier this year, though. Married man." She giggled and stared off into the distance at something only she could see. Looking back at Creed, she added, "Funny that I should recall that about him. I usually don't remember much about the men who pass through these doors unless they're regulars."

The curiosity that had drawn him to this woman in the first place jolted Creed with a suspicion. Thinking to take a shot in the dark, he asked, "His name wasn't Marshall Quade, was it?"

Addie shrugged and said, "Could have been. I don't rightly recollect. I only recall that he was from Texas and his new bride wasn't as friendly in the dark as she was in the light, if you know what I mean."

"New bride?"

"That's what he said, I think." She thought about it for a second. "Yep. That's what he said all right."

"But you can't recall his name?"

"No, I can't." Her brow furrowed. "Why are you so interested in this man, Mr. Creed?"

"That's a long story, Miss LaMont."

"I got time to burn, Mr. Creed. Why don't you come inside and tell me all about it?"

"That's a mighty tempting offer, Miss LaMont, but I must decline at this time. I've got too many other matters on my mind right now, and quite frankly, all of them involve women."

Addie grinned lasciviously and said, "Yes, I'll bet they do."

Creed cleared his throat and said, "About this fellow with the new bride? You can't recall anything else about him, can you? Besides him being a Texan, I mean."

"Well, let me think about that for a minute. I remember him saying that he was from Texas, but his bride was from Tennessee, and they'd come to Denver looking to set up housekeeping, but he wasn't having much luck finding work that suited him."

"That sounds like Marsh Quade," said Creed. "And you say he lives here in Denver?"

"No, I didn't say that. If I recollect right, he said something about trying his luck at prospecting." She giggled again. "I remember laughing when he said that because he'd just got through telling me about not finding work that suited him. I don't think he knew how tough hunting for gold can be. He said he was thinking about going up to Central City from here."

"Central City? Where's that from here?"

Addie pointed west and said, "Up there. In those mountains. You just ride in that direction and you'll find it." She studied Creed for another second, then added, "Are you sure you don't want to come in for that drink?"

"Maybe some other time, Miss LaMont." He waved his hat at her in a gallant gesture and added, "I thank you for the information, ma'am, and as they say in New Orleans, *Adieu, mon cher*." He spurred Nimbus and headed back through the city, crossing the Blake Street bridge into West Denver and taking the ferry across the South Platte River to Highlands. He picked up the stagecoach road there and followed it to Golden where he spent the night, and the next morning he road up the mountain trail to Central City.

11

William Green Russell's 1858 discovery of gold in the South Platte River Valley started a major shift of the population to the Territories.

John Gregory's greater strike in the mountains the following spring added impetus to the flow of immigrants to the western regions of Kansas Territory.

News of these two events spread rapidly across the nation through the newspapers, but the real clincher that ensured the Americanization of the Rockies was the prose of William Byers, the publisher of *The Rocky Mountain News*, and Jonathan Kellom, the Superintendent of Public Instruction of Nebraska. Kellom and Byers authored a small book entitled *Hand Book to the Gold Fields of Nebraska and Kansas*. In their opening statement to the reader, they wrote:

"It is not the object of this work to persuade you to go to the recently discovered Nebraska and Kansas Gold Mines, but to lay before you a mass of testimony and information whereby you may be able to make a judicious decision; when and if you decide to go, we propose to assist you by information which will be useful to you in procuring your outfit, and determining the route by which you will travel."

They lied. Their whole purpose of publishing the book was to persuade its readers to drop everything and rush off to the

Rockies to search for gold, and if they did, they should go by way of Council Bluffs, Iowa, and Omaha, Nebraska Territory, because several businesses in those burgeoning twin cities on the Missouri River supported the book with paid advertising. Wisely, the authors published their book in that new metropolis of the West, Chicago, and the local newsmen co-operated completely with front-page articles in their tabloids, aiding and abetting the cause with embellishments of their own.

Seasoned prospectors realized early on that Russell's discovery in the valley was only a tease, that Gregory's find on Vasquez Creek was the true lode, and that they should make the climb into the mountains if they too should have any chance at striking it rich. The result was Central City and a plethora of satellite communities possessing varying degrees of civility and stability: Black Hawk, Mountain City, Springfield, Missouri City, Bortonsburg, Eureka, and Nevada City.

Sometimes known as Gregory Gulch or Gregory's Diggins or just plain Gregory, Mountain City was the first of the towns to grow up with very little direction or purpose around the Gregory claims. Black Hawk and Central City developed to the east and west of Mountain City respectively. Eureka sprung out of the discovery of gold in Eureka Gulch by Harry Gunnell who announced his find by yelling, "Eureka! Eureka! I have found it!" Springfield, Bortonsburg, and Missouri City resulted merely from miners pitching their tents in close proximity to some enterprising fellow with a keg of whiskey who set up a tent saloon in their midst.

Nevada City, the most westerly and the noisiest of the satellite towns, evolved a mile up Nevada Creek from Central City. The name, Nevada City, stuck in the minds of the miners, but the Post Office Department in distant Washington had other thoughts. The Postmaster General made the official name of the town Nevadaville in order to distinguish it from two other places named Nevada City—one in Montana and the other in Nevada.

Whether as Nevada City or Nevadaville, the community was best known for the thirteen saloons that fronted its one-block Main Street, all of them built from unpainted rough-cut lumber. The largest of these was Maxwell Hall which boasted a second story where stage entertainments were held; everything from the song-and-dance routines of the fabled Mike Dougherty to traveling thespians performing their favorite Shakespearean play. When the upper level wasn't being used for theatrical ventures, the management stacked the benches in such a way as to make temporary walls for the purpose of renting makeshift rooms to overnight guests.

The sign proclaiming the establishment as a hostelry of sorts attracted Creed to the Maxwell. He took such a room for himself and boarded Nimbus in the stable behind the saloon. Hungry, he repaired to the bar for an expensive supper. While standing at the rail minding his own business, consuming a small repast of a roast beef sandwich, hard-boiled egg, and a beer, he overheard a conversation that aroused his curiosity and alerted him to a danger that he'd confronted all too often since the end of the War Between the States.

Stationed near Creed, leaning on the bar and quaffing beer that was brewed in Denver, were two fellows of ordinary appearance. One wore a maroon coat, brown trousers, boots, and a low-crown hat with the brim pushed back. He was clean shaven with the exception of a thin black mustache. The other man's attire consisted of a faded blue shirt, denim trousers, high-top work shoes, and a plainsman hat. He sported a full set of black chin whiskers and mustache.

"I heard tell that they're Rebs," said the first gent. "One's supposed to be a Texan. The rest are supposed to be from Missouri. Guerrillas who rode with Quantrill and Bloody Bill Anderson and Arch Clement and the like. Some are from

Kentucky and Tennessee. Murdering, thieving Rebs, all of them."

That was the statement that caught Creed's ear.

"I heard the same thing," said the second, alcohol slurring his words. "They're supposed to be holed up in the Snowy Range. They ride down from there every so often and hold up some honest working man who's not doing anything except trying to scratch a living from the ground. Just like they did when they shot John Williams and robbed him and his brother. Then they ride back up into the mountains and hide from the law. Good Union men, those Williams brothers. Damn shame about John."

"We ought to get up a bunch of good Union men and ride up there and roust those boys out of the country."

"Goddamn Rebel bastards! They didn't learn nothing from the war, did they? I think we ought to ride up there, catch the dirty bastards, and string them up to the nearest tree. That'll teach those Rebs who really won the war."

"Hanging's too good for them. We ought to get up a real good bunch of Union men and have us a tar-and-feather party. Ride every Reb in the territory out of this country on a rail. If they can't live peaceably in this country, then they don't deserve to live here at all. We ought to run them all back to the South where they belong."

"That's right, we should."

"Damn Southerners."

"Now they're not all bad. Let's not forget that John Gregory and Green Russell were Southerners, and if it weren't for them finding the first gold in these parts, we might not be here. Both came from Georgia, I heard."

"I heard the same. But that was before the war. You don't see either one of them around these parts no more, do you?" When his compatriot didn't reply immediately, the man answered his own question. "No, you don't. Gregory up and disappeared, and Russell high-tailed it back to the Indian nations to fight for the South. Just as well. He wasn't nothing but a half-breed Cherokee anyway. And a Rebel to boot."

"Well, they're just two less for us good Union men to deal with in these parts."

"That's right."

"But why should we care about those bastards? Billy Cozens is out looking for them right now with a posse."

"If anybody can catch those thieving varmints, it's Billy Cozens. Damn good sheriff, that Billy. He'll catch the bastards for sure."

"Yep, he will."

"Then we'll hang 'em."

"Yep, we will."

Suddenly, a fight broke out between players in a poker game at a corner table. One man pulled a Bowie knife, and the other drew a derringer. The second gambler shot the first in the stomach, but the bullet failed to save him from the big blade driven deep into his chest. He screamed in pain, stumbled toward the door with the knife protruding from the right of his sternum, dropped to his knees before he reached the exit, and muttered, "I'm killed. Don't tell my mother how I died. It'd break her old heart." Clutching the Bowie, he fell face forward onto the dirty floor, dead.

The victim of the gunshot held his hands over his bloody bullet wound, watching his assailant die. "Serves the sonofabitch right," he yelled loudly. "He's killed me, too. I'm glad I killed the cheating sonofabitch." He slumped back into his chair. "Somebody get me a drink. If I'm gonna die, I'll do it feeling no pain."

Somebody sent for a doctor, but the dying man would have no part of that. He drank and bled, bled and drank, bled and died.

"Well, that's Nevadaville luck for you," said the drunk with chin whiskers.

"Yep," said the other. "Nevadaville luck. You think you struck a mother lode, and it turns out to be just a pocket. All for nothing."

The two men drank up and staggered from the saloon.

Creed stayed until the finish, although he knew that the man would die like so many other fools who acted without forethought, who placed themselves in untenable positions, who allowed themselves to be trapped like the coyote that has to gnaw off its own leg to be free again. He went to his room thinking that he might also be one of those fools. I just wonder which leg I'll have to gnaw off first, he thought as he retired for the night.

Shortly before dawn the next morning Creed rode out of Nevadaville, taking the trail that circled around Alps Mountain to the town of Russell Gulch. Just outside of town, as first light glimmered in the east, he came upon a tent community of miners who were stirring to begin another day of hard labor in the mines, whether their own or somebody else's. He recognized two of them as the men that he'd overheard in Maxwell's the night before. His intention was to ride on by, but when they hailed him to pause at their camp, he had no other choice but to accept their hospitality.

"Morning, friend," said the man wearing the same maroon coat that he'd worn the night before. He was making biscuits and placing them in a pie pan next to the fire. "Had your breakfast yet?" He put the last biscuit in the pan, dusted flour from his hands, and stood up.

"Thought I'd wait a spell before eating today," said Creed, remaining atop Nimbus.

"That's not good, friend. A man needs a full belly to face the long day ahead. Climb down and sit yourself by the fire.

We got plenty of coffee and biscuits and bacon. You're more than welcome to join us."

"I thank you for the invite, sir, but I really should be riding along."

"Nonsense," said the other man Creed had seen and heard the night before. He was cutting slices of bacon from a two-inch thick slab and putting them in the frying pan beside the fire. "You heard what Jack said. You can't do much on an empty stomach, so climb down and join us for breakfast."

Creed forced a friendly smile and said, "I don't see how I can rightly refuse when you put it like that." He climbed down, tied Nimbus to a tent stake, and joined the two miners by the fire.

"Coffee?" asked the one named Jack. He held out a tin cup of steaming coffee to Creed.

"Thank you," said the Texan, taking the cup. He sniffed the rich, black brew and remarked, "Sure smells good, friend."

"The name is Jack Burch, and this fellow is Bill Rust. We're from St. Joe County, Indiana." He knelt down beside the fire.

"I am Slate Creed from Lavaca County, Texas."

Rust and Burch eyed each other warily for a second, then looked back at Creed.

The bacon sizzled in the frying pan. The odors from the cooking meat and baking biscuits were delicious and enticing. They stirred memories of other mornings in Creed's past, gentle, peaceful mornings such as this one was so far.

"Oh, you're a Southerner," said Burch.

Creed tensed for an instant, then dropped to one knee. "No, I'm a Texan," he said.

"What's the difference?" asked Rust.

Creed smiled and said, "I suppose you'd have to be a Texan to know the answer to that one."

"You Texans gave us a lot of hell during the war," said Burch. "Did you fight for the Confederacy?"

"No, I fought for Texas and the right to live as I please without some fool politician a thousand miles away making my decisions for me. What were you fighting for?"

"I was doing my patriotic duty to preserve the Union that you Rebs were trying to destroy," said Burch.

"When the game turns crooked," said Creed, staring purposely into his cup, "a fellow has the right to throw down his cards and get out, doesn't he?"

"That's cards, not politics," said Burch. "We were all one country before Jeff Davis and his friends tried to split us up."

Creed pinpointed his gaze on Burch and said evenly, "That much I will agree on, sir. Looking back now, I see that the plantation owners brought on the war by trying to preserve a way of life that shouldn't have ever begun in the first place."

"Are you telling me that you were opposed to slavery, Mr. Creed?" inquired Rust.

"I am grievously opposed to it now, but before the war, I can't say that I ever gave it much thought. We had slaves on our plantation down in Texas, but we didn't treat them like slaves. Leastways, not like most slave owners treated their slaves. My grandfathers taught me to think of Negroes as people who deserved to be treated with the same regard that you give any other person—white, black, or red. My grandfather Dougald Slater bought several slaves, but he never sold any. He let them marry and have children, but he never split up any families. He allowed the men with families an acre of land to grow extra food for themselves, and if they grew more than they needed, he let them sell the extra produce in town, and he let them keep the money, too. Whenever a slave saved up enough money that was equal to half of what my grandfather paid for him, he could buy his freedom and his family's freedom. I wasn't there when my grandfather died, but I was told that he freed all of his slaves in his will." He thought of Hannah and her family. "When I returned from the war, nearly all the Negroes were gone. Only a few house servants remained."

"But you still fought for the South," repeated Burch.

"Mr. Burch, the war is over," said Creed. "Why don't we leave it at that?"

"Agreed," said Rust firmly.

"Agreed," said Burch reluctantly.

"Where are you headed this fine morning, Mr. Creed?" inquired Rust.

"Into the mountains," said Creed.

"Hell, you're already in the mountains," smirked Burch.

"Are you prospecting?" asked Rust.

"No, I'm just looking for some place to be alone. I've had my fill of towns, and I'd like to find some peace and quiet for a spell."

"Can't say that I blame you there," said Rust. "If I didn't have my heart set on marrying Jack's sister Ella back in Indiana, I think I'd ride off just like you're doing, Mr. Creed, but I need to scrape up enough gold to buy a proper farm back home where Ella and me can raise up a family."

"You know, Mr. Rust, I sort of envy you for that."

"Why's that, Mr. Creed?"

"You've got a home to go back to."

Rust and Burch exchanged looks again, then looked back at Creed as he placed his cup on the ground near the pot.

"Would you like some more, Mr. Creed?" asked Rust.

"No, thank you," said Creed. He stood up. "I think I'd best be riding on now. Thanks for the coffee, Mr. Burch, Mr. Rust."

"You can't go yet," said Rust, standing up, too. "The biscuits and bacon ain't ready yet."

Burch also stood.

"Thank you, but I'd better go now. I might have a long ride ahead of me." He tipped his hat to them. "I hope you get enough gold for that farm, Mr. Rust. Good luck to you both." He untied Nimbus, mounted up, and rode away.

"Strange bird, don't you think, Jack?" said Rust as he and Burch watched Creed disappear down the trail.

"A Reb. That says it all, Bill. Come on. Let's eat. We got a hard day ahead of us." He knelt again and helped himself to a biscuit and a slice of bacon.

Rust continued to stare after Creed. "You don't think he's one of those that Billy Cozens is chasing, do you, Jack?"

"Well, one of them outlaws is a Texan," said Burch. "He might be the one. Who knows for sure? Come on and eat some breakfast, Bill."

"What do you think he meant by that remark about us having a home to go back to?"

"How the hell should I know?" groused Burch. "What's more, I don't care. Come on and eat and forget about that Reb, will you?"

That's easier said than done, thought Rust as he joined Burch on the ground again.

12

"And today you found Ouray," the Indian said as Creed concluded his tale.

Creed snorted a laugh, a cloud of breath billowing before him in the flickering firelight. "Yes," he said, "I suppose you could put it that way. Although I'd say it's more like you found me."

The Ute nodded slowly and said softly, "*Sí,* Ouray found Creed." He pinpointed a stare on Creed's eyes as an elfin smile curled the corners of his own mouth.

Creed interpreted the grin on his companion's face as a sign of cunning, as a false front for the truth. Suspecting the Indian of hiding something from him, he said, "All right, Ouray, now it's your turn to speak."

"No, Ouray will not speak tonight." He stretched out on the bed of pine boughs that he'd made for himself and covered up with the elk robe that he'd brought along as the only creature comfort on his vision quest. "*Mañana, mi amigo. Mañana.*"

"*¿Mañana?*"

"*Mañana,*" reiterated Ouray. "We sleep now." He rolled over, turning his back to the Texan.

Creed shook his head, thinking, Tomorrow! It's always tomorrow with Mexicans, but he's an Indian. How do you figure them? Hm-m, he thought. Maybe they've got something

there. Life is too damn short to be cramming everything into
today. He followed Ouray's example and slipped between the
blankets of his bedroll. Maybe tomorrow will be a better day
for doing what you could have done today. Sure, tomorrow.
It can wait. He can tell me his story tomorrow. I'll be looking
forward to it. I'll . . .

He drifted off to sleep.

The sun rose with unusual brilliance and warmth the next
morning, inspiring the birds to sing with additional clarity and
verve and the squirrels to play in the treetops, chattering bois-
terously. The wildlife symphony awakened Creed gradually,
stirring a sweet dream of home in his mind as he made the
transition from deep sleep to wakefulness.

He dreamt that he walked hand in hand with Texada along
a stream that flowed into the Lavaca River. Spring adorned
Texas. The fields bloomed with bluebonnets, and their per-
fume permeated the air. A small boy skipped stones across
the creek. Joy filled Creed as he took Texada into his arms
and kissed her. She was so lovely. Flaxen hair falling to her
shoulders, pavonine eyes, and tawny complexion. How he
loved her! He felt a tug at his trousers. He looked down
at the small boy. The child had his brother Dent's face.
He smiled up at Creed and said, "Massuh Clete! Massuh
Clete! Watch me, Massuh Clete! Watch me throw this
stone." Creed watched as the boy's skin turned darker and
darker until he was no longer little Dent, until he became
a—

Creed came awake with a start. That's what I have to do,
he thought. He shook his head. What? Do what? He sat up
abruptly and rubbed his eyes as the light of day finally pen-
etrated his senses. Not really seeing anything around him yet,
he considered the dream just concluded. Texada, he thought.
Oh, darling, how I miss you! A ravenous yearning gnawed
the pit of his stomach.

He recalled the boy with his brother's face that had turned into the face of a slave child. He let his head droop with sadness as he thought about Dent. Tears came to his eyes. He was so young, he thought. Too young to die. He didn't deserve to die. If I'd only gotten there sooner, I might have saved him. I might have taken that bullet for him, and he'd be alive today. Maybe we'd both be better off if I had. He wiped his eyes on the sleeve of his shirt.

Get a grip on yourself, son, he thought. He sniffed, cleared his throat, and spit. Dent's dead, and there's nothing you can do to bring him back. Then the light exploded in his head. But I can do something for his son. His head bobbed as a smile spread over his face. Yes, I can do something for his son. He threw off the blanket and jumped to his feet. Yes, I can do something for Little Dent. He smiled broadly, but it didn't last.

A quick scan of the camp revealed that something was amiss. Nimbus was gone. So was Ouray.

"Damn! That sonofabitching Indian stole my horse!" He looked around for his guns and saw his saddle, saddlebags, rifle, and scabbard exactly where he'd put them the night before. He saw his hat, bent over, and picked it up to find that his Colt's and Bowie were still beneath it. He grabbed the six-gun, checked the loads, donned the hat, and stormed off to search for signs of Nimbus and Ouray. He didn't have to go far.

"Buenos dias, mi amigo," said Ouray, hailing Creed from a distance through the trees. He walked slowly toward the Texan. "You slept well, Creed?"

"I slept fine, you sonofabitching thief," snapped Creed. He stopped and leveled his Colt's at the Ute. "Where the hell is my horse?"

Ouray halted in his tracks and took on the aspect of a warrior refusing to show his emotions to an enemy.

Creed recognized the blankness in Ouray's eyes as the same expression that Grandfather Hawk McConnell had taught him as a boy. "Do not let your enemy see what you feel inside," he'd said on so many occasions, "and he can never harm you." Wise counsel. Seeing the emptiness in the Ute's face and slowly realizing that nothing else was missing, the Texan felt a tinge of shame, lowered the revolver, and said calmly, "Where's my horse, my friend?"

"Ouray staked him in the meadow beyond these trees," said Ouray. "The grass is plentiful there."

Creed nodded and said, "Thank you."

Ouray smiled and said, "You would have done the same for Ouray's horse . . . if Ouray had one."

"That's right. You don't have a horse. Why not?"

"Ouray has horses. Many horses. But Ouray does not have one with him on this journey. It is not the way."

"Yes, your journey. Your quest for a vision. Will you tell me about it today?"

Ouray moved closer to Creed and said, "Yes, Ouray will tell you today, but first we eat."

They prepared a breakfast of venison cooked in bacon grease, fried biscuits, and coffee. As they ate, Ouray related his tale in the fashion peculiar to Indians.

"My father was a great chief, and my mother was a beautiful woman but also a slave because she was a mixed-blood of Apache and Mexican. Because my father loved her so much, he forsook his people and went to live in the Mexican town of Taos. I was raised there and in Santa Fe. I learned the Mexican and American tongues there.

"When my father died, I became a chief. This is not the way that most young men become chiefs. Most must earn their right to be called chief. I became a chief because of my wealth. My father gave me many horses before he died.

I returned to my people when they fought the war with the Americans who gave our war chiefs the smallpox coats. That was twelve years ago. We killed many Americans, but they won the war because we did not have the guns or the food to sustain us.

"I learned then that there are many more Americans than there are *Nuche,* and there is nothing my people can do to stop them from coming to our country. When the white men found gold in these mountains, I knew that more Americans would come here and soon the *Nuche* would be without a country. I have seen the city they call Denver. I have seen the city they call Central. These are places that will not go away.

"I have come to the high mountains many times before seeking a vision, and each time I have seen the other side. Manitou has shown me the time yet to come, and each time I have seen that the *Nuche* are only red leaves in the white wind of the Americans. We are powerless to stop them. They come and kill us, and we kill them for this, but they come more and more and kill us more and more. We kill them, but still they come. I have learned that the *Nuche* must live in peace with the Americans, or soon the Americans will kill all of us and we will be no more.

"I have tried to teach my people this, but too many chiefs tell them that it is better to die fighting than to die starving. They say that there is no honor in a slow death. I must agree with them, but I must argue that we can live in peace with the Americans if we stay away from them, if we move away to the mountains where there is no gold. We have done this, but still the Americans come into our country looking for gold. We tell them there is none there, but they do not believe us. We tell them to look for the gold, find it, take it, and leave. Do not build your houses in our country. They do not listen, so I came to the high mountains again to seek a new vision. I hoped that Manitou would show me how to convince the white men to leave us alone in our own country. Manitou has given me a new vision. And in this vision, Ouray has seen the other side of tomorrow."

"And what did you see this time, Ouray?"

The Ute smiled, shook his head, and said, "Ouray has spoken enough, Creed. It is Creed's turn to speak again. What will Creed do now?"

"Oh, no, you don't, *jefe*. You don't tell me that much and not finish the story."

"To tell you more would be bad medicine, *mi amigo*. It would change the time yet to come."

"Change the future? How can that be when the future isn't even here yet?"

"Ouray does not know. Ouray only knows that the future Ouray saw would be changed if Ouray tells you about it."

"If you tell me about it?" He squinted at the Indian. "Was I in your future, Ouray?"

Slowly, the Ute said, "Ouray has spoken enough, Now it is Creed's turn to speak. What will you do now, Creed?"

Creed stared hard at Ouray, wondering why the Indian refused to answer his question. Finally, he understood. He drank the last of the coffee in his cup, wiped his mouth on his coat sleeve, and said, "I don't know exactly, but I can tell you this much. I'm gonna see that my brother's son is raised right. That's the least I can do for him."

"Him?"

"Him?"

"Yes, him. Which him do you speak of?"

Creed thought for a few seconds, then said, "Actually, both of them. It's the least I can do for them."

"Ouray understands. How will you see that the child is raised right?"

"I'm not sure yet," said Creed, "but I do know that the first thing I have to do is get Little Dent and his mother out of that saloon in Denver. That's no place for a woman to raise a child."

"You do not care that the child's mother was once a slave?"

Creed hesitated a mere second before answering. "No, I don't."

Ouray nodded. "Now you are seeing with your heart again, *mi amigo*. This is good. What else will you do now?"

"What do you mean?"

"The man that you hunt. What about him?"

"Oh, you mean Marsh Quade."

"Yes, Quade."

"I'm not sure yet. I've heard stories that lead me to believe that he's one of those outlaws the sheriff is hunting with a posse. After what he did with Blackburn and the others, I suppose it's not hard to believe that Quade's turned completely to thievery. I don't know. I suppose I'll look up his wife while I'm in Denver and see if she can tell me where I might find Quade. If she can't, maybe I'll go hunting him myself."

"And when you find him, will you harm him?"

"No. No, I won't do that. I need him to tell the soldiers the truth so I can be a free man again."

Ouray nodded and said, "You are ready to return to your people now. Ouray will go with you as far as Central City."

"Why do you want to go there?" asked Creed.

Ouray hesitated a moment, then smiled and said, "Whiskey."

13

Nevadaville was in an uproar when Creed and Ouray entered the town three days later. The Texan rode, while the Ute trotted beside him.

Main Street teemed with men of all sorts, though most were miners who had left the mines in the middle of the day for more important business in town. They stood in the street, on the sidewalks, and in the saloons, all bunched in knots of five or more, conversing with animated agitation. A trio of words—outlaws, Texan, and hanging—resounded commonly from their excited discourses, the unnatural combination alarming Creed, warning him to move with the caution of a cat on glare ice.

Creed reined in Nimbus in front of Maxwell Hall, where a clot of men stood to each side of the doorway. The Texan dismounted slowly and surveyed the scene with his new friend. "I don't like the looks of this, Ouray," he said. "It feels bad here."

"Yes, very bad," said the Ute. "Maybe Creed and Ouray should not be here."

"You might have something there, *amigo,* but let's find out what's happening here before we do anything hasty." He hitched the appaloosa to the rail, stepped onto the boardwalk, and started to enter the saloon. When he noticed that Ouray wasn't following him, he stopped, turned, and said, "Aren't you coming with me?"

"This is not a good place for Ouray, *mi amigo*. At the end of the street is Pedro's Cantina. Ouray is welcome there. Ouray will go there now and wait for you." He untied his elk robe from the horse's haunches, smiled at Creed, and added, "And the whiskey is better at Pedro's." He winked and headed off toward the cantina.

"Wait. I'll go with you."

Ouray stopped, turned back to Creed, and said, "No, you must go alone now. Ouray will be at Pedro's when you need him. Whenever that time will be, Ouray will be there. But for now, Creed must go alone." Sure that Creed wouldn't follow, he started for the cantina again.

Creed didn't quite understand, but he remained on the boardwalk, watching the Ute walk down the street. He did notice how nobody paid any attention to the Indian carrying the elk robe. It's almost like he's invisible, thought Creed.

A fellow shouting, "Hang the bastards!" returned Creed's focus to the current circumstance. He took a sidestep to enter the saloon and bumped into a miner hurrying to join his friends up the street. "Beg your pardon, sir," he said.

"Yeah, sure," said the man, eager to be moving on.

Intentionally blocking the fellow's path, Creed said, "Excuse me for asking, but I just rode into town from a hunting trip in the mountains." He waved at the crowded thoroughfare. "What's all the fuss about here?"

Wild-eyed with bloodthirsty hysteria, the fellow chortled, "Sheriff Cozens caught those outlaws that killed John Williams last week. There's gonna be a hanging." He laughed sadistically and bounded away.

A lynching, you mean, thought Creed, gazing after the man. He'd seen lynch mobs before, and the sight sickened him. Everybody gone mad. Damn fools! Every man deserves a fair trial, and if he's found guilty and the seriousness of the crime calls for it, then—and only then—does he deserve to hang. Nobody has the right to deny a man a fair trial. Not in this country. As much as he wanted to say his piece on the subject, he knew it wouldn't do him any better than pissing into the wind. Men bent on vengeance made a poor audience for a speaker of reason.

Again, Creed heard the three catch words that bothered him: outlaws, Texan, and hanging. Quade! Is Marshall Quade the Texan? he wondered. What if he is? What do I do then? Whoa, boy! First things first. Find out if this Texan is Marsh Quade before you start thinking of what it might mean to you.

Creed scanned the street and thought he recognized Jack Burch and Bill Rust in a group of men across the way. He sauntered over to them and bent an ear to their talk.

"He caught the whole lot of them," said Burch. "Dirty Rebs, all of them. They gotta hang. That's all those bastards understand." He noticed Creed standing at the periphery of the crowd. "What are you doing here, Reb?"

All eyes turned on Creed.

"Easy, Jack," said Rust. "He ain't one of them that Billy was chasing."

"He's a Reb, ain't he?"

"No, sir, I'm not," said Creed, feeling the need to defend himself. "I'm an American just like you men."

"Not like me, you ain't," said Burch. "I fought for the Stars and Stripes, not the Stars and Bars like you did."

"That's all in the past," said Creed, "and that's where it's gonna stay."

"That's right, Reb, it's in the past, but it ain't gonna stay there. Not as long as you Rebs keep forgetting who won the war."

"Don't you mean as long as men like you keep reminding us who won the war?"

Burch's face pinched up around his eyes as he said, "That's right, you dirty sonofabitch."

Creed's face took on the aspect of the Choctaw warrior within him. "Mr. Burch, I know you're all excited over these outlaws—"

"You're damn right, we are, Reb," interjected Burch.

"—and in times like this, a fellow is likely to say things he wouldn't say otherwise."

"Do you mean like calling you a dirty sonofabitch, you dirty sonofabitch?"

"Exactly right, Mr. Burch. Excitement or not, you have no call to use that word in conjunction with me."

"In conwhat?" sputtered Burch. "What are you, some sort of educated wise-ass?"

"It means you have no reason to use that word on me," said Creed.

"Yes, I do, you dirty sonofabitch. You're a Reb, and all Rebs are sonofabitching bastards in my book."

"Mr. Burch, I will ask you to apologize just one time, and—"

"And what if I won't do it, Reb? Then what?"

Other groups of men noticed the confrontation developing between Creed and Burch, and they began moving closer to them.

Creed no longer hesitated to react to Burch's insult. He drew his Colt's, cocked it, and took aim at the man's belligerent face. "Then I will shoot you dead," he said, his aspect as calm as an undertaker dressing a body for burial. When a few of the other men made movements as though they might try to intervene, he added, "I have five balls in this Colt's .44-caliber cap-and-ball revolver, and I am a dead shot. I can kill five men before any one of you can draw his weapon." He paused intentionally. "The question is, which five will die?"

Nobody moved except Rust. He raised his hands in front of him and said, "Now hold on everybody. There's no need for any of this." He turned to his friend. "Jack, you owe Mr. Creed an apology."

"The hell you say!" snapped Burch.

"Yes, I do say!" growled Rust right back at him. "This man has done nothing to deserve being called something so foul."

"He's a Reb, Bill."

"The war is over, Jack. Put it to rest."

"Listen to your friend, Mr. Burch," said Creed. "He's speaking good sense. The war is over, and the quicker every man puts it behind him, the better off we'll all be."

The other men in the group muttered and mumbled various sounds of agreement with Creed and Rust.

"I still don't like Rebs," said Burch, "but I suppose I shouldn't have called you a sonofabitch, Mr. Creed."

"I'll take that as an apology, Mr. Burch," said Creed. He uncocked his Colt's, but he didn't replace it inside his waistband, as a precaution against further trouble. "Mr. Burch, I don't like outlaws any more than you do, and I particularly don't like other Texans giving my state a bad name. I'm just as glad as you are that the sheriff caught these outlaws, and as for the Texan among them, I'd like to find out who he is just so I can tell his kinfolk back home what happened to him up here in Colorado."

"Well, we don't know what his name is yet," said Burch, "but we'll be sure to ask him just before we string him up. Ain't that right, boys?"

A murmur of agreement came from the other men.

Creed recalled his thoughts about lynch mobs and decided he was right, Nothing he could say would deter this bunch from carrying out their plans. He saw only one course of action.

"Well, you men do what you have to do," said Creed. "As for me, I want no part of a lynching."

"That figures," said Burch.

"Leave it alone, Jack," said Rust. "You go on about your business, Mr. Creed, and we'll do the same. Fair enough?"

"Fair enough," said Creed. Tipping his hat, he added, "Gents." Still holding his gun at his side, he backed away slowly toward Maxwell Hall.

"Let's get back to business," said Burch.

Other small groups of men gathered around Burch to hear him instigate mob action.

Creed watched and listened for a few minutes from the boardwalk in front of Maxwell Hall, then quietly he mounted Nimbus and rode off toward Central City.

14

Billy Cozens was a '59er, arriving that Colorado Gold Rush year in Black Hawk nearly broke and looking for work. He hired on with Jack Kehler who owned a store and saloon. Cozens clerked and tended bar, and when Kehler was made the district sheriff by the miners, Cozens was appointed his first deputy. Two years later when Gilpin County became an official geographical locality, William Z. Cozens was elected its first sheriff.

Six-foot-two, handsome, and affable, Cozens enforced the law with a gentle hand more often than not, but when the occasion called for it, he could be as hard as the rock that the miners hammered and chipped and blasted every working day for the gold that it jealously guarded. He relished the work because it took him all over the mine-pocked county on horseback and because it paid so well, the times being when a sheriff made commissions for performing his duties as tax collector, process server, and debt collector.

Cozens married Mary York, the first American woman to settle in Gregory Gulch, having been brought there by Green Russell who had found her alone on the prairie.

Mary York was twelve years old when she immigrated to Canada from Ireland in 1842 with her parents who died shortly thereafter. Plain and untrained in social graces, she supported herself as a domestic maid for the next seventeen years in Canada, New York City, and Baltimore, where she worked for the McGees. When her employers invited her to accompany them to the Pike's Peak region of Kansas Territory, Mary saw the chance to find a husband and a future. She accepted. While crossing the Plains, Mr. McGee made a lewd advance toward Mary, causing her to flee in order to protect and preserve her virtue.

She came upon Russell as he prospected along the Platte River on his return to Colorado in the spring of 1859, and after explaining her plight, he took her under his care and protection, allowing her to mend and wash the clothes of his men for her keep. When they arrived in Gregory Gulch, Russell set her up in her own cabin and in her own business as a cook, laundress, and seamstress, and although she was the only woman in the camp for some time to come, she had no serious suitors until Billy Cozens. Even he wasn't that serious until they were actually wed.

Gilpin County had no jail in its earliest days, and how it came to have one was a tale that Cozens delighted in relating at every opportunity.

"Well, you know what trouble we'd been having trying to establish law and order in these parts in the early days," he'd say, "and how if we caught a man stealing a horse or robbing gold out of a sluice box, we had a pretty speedy trial by a committee, and we'd string him up or run him out of the country? Well, before we got our court working, that wasn't so bad. But when Governor Gilpin appointed three commissioners for Gilpin County, seemed like we should begin to do better than that.

"Not long after, I picked up two husky horse thieves late one afternoon and had to keep them in custody until court would open in the morning. And here I was with no jail and no place to put them. So I took them home—right into Mrs. Cozens's bedroom. She was still in bed, for our son Willie had just been born a few days before.

"When I tell you that she didn't like it, I mean she didn't like it. She wasn't mealy-mouthed about what she had to say to me, either. I told her I was in a hell of a fix, that I had to keep those men in our house because I had no other place to put them.

"Well, I chained them both to the bedpost at the foot of her bed and told them to lay down on the floor. Then I took out my revolver and shook it in their faces and said to them, 'You fellows keep quiet now—mind you keep damn quiet, too, for if you disturb that baby or my wife, I'll shoot you.' Of course, I wouldn't ever have done such a thing, but I managed to make them believe I would.

"Morning came, and those men had never stirred an inch, nor made a squeal of any kind.

"But Mrs. Cozens opened fire on me plenty. She notified me that she wouldn't stand it, said it was an outrage to turn her bedroom into a jail to shelter pesky horse thieves, that never again would such a thing happen in her house, and that it wouldn't have happened this time if she'd been strong enough to stand on her feet.

"Well, I gathered that she meant it. It made me realize something would have to be done about a jail, and after I had turned my prisoners over to the court bailiff, I started out to hunt up county commissioners. I rounded them up in the next hour or so and asked them to hold an important meeting right away. They did, and I told them the whole story and said how hard it was to be a sheriff without a jail.

"The chairman said, 'Billy, we know damn well you ought to have a jail, but just now the county government hasn't any money and we can't do a thing for you.'

" 'Oh, yes, you can,' I said. 'You've got to. I know you

have no county money, but right now you do this thing in a lawful way. Have the board enter an order that the sheriff build a jail, and authorize him to employ county prisoners upon the work. All you need to do is to run the county in debt for a little lime, a few bars of iron, some planks, and nails. I'll go out and find the necessary prisoners to build the damn jail.'

"Well, such an order was entered on the records, and I started work. There were a lot of bad ones loafing around camp that I'd come to know pretty well. They all knew about the new law officers being appointed, and they weren't at all anxious to have them start digging in past records. You know, you can do a lot with that kind of man if you go at him right—he's afraid of you. I rounded up quite a bunch of them and told them the county commissioners weren't gonna stand for a lot of dirty bums loafing around the camp and they had to go to work in my chain gang. Some of them rustled stone, others mixed mortar, and some masons among them laid the walls. When I needed a carpenter or a blacksmith on the job, I simply rounded up one.

"Well, some of them fellows wanted to get up an argument about their rights. I said, 'Now be calm about this. You know damn well what you are wanted for back in the States. I don't think you are so big a fool as to want to pick a fuss with the officers of the law over a few days' work. If you're intending to stay around these diggings, there won't be no fuss.' They saw that I held all the aces.

"Well, we finished that jail pretty damn quick. We had to. Mrs. Cozens was well and on her feet again."

On four different occasions, Cozens had stood on the steps of that jail and artfully fended off an angry crowd in a lynching mood. Once, after hiding his prisoner in the shaft of the Casey Mine as an extra measure of safety, Cozens pleaded with the citizens not to besmirch the good reputation of Central City as a law-abiding community, and the mob dispersed. The sheriff's success was due as much to the town's natural disposition to be orderly as to his own force of character. Central City's calmness influenced neighboring Mountain City and Black Hawk to a similar respect for the law, but not so Nevadaville, where the statutes had a tendency to bend severely in the winds of vice.

Cozens knew this fact all too well, and for that reason, his jail was an armed fortress when Creed rode up to it that August afternoon. "Just hold it right there, stranger," said Cozens, a double-barrelled shotgun draped over his left arm and a .44-caliber Colt's strapped to his right hip. "Who are you and what business do you have here?"

"I'm Slate Creed from Lavaca County, Texas, and I'm looking for the sheriff. Would you be him?"

"Yes, I am. What can I do for you?"

"Well, sir, it's more of what I can do for you."

"How's that?" asked Cozens, now quite curious.

"I'm just now coming from Nevadaville, Sheriff, and I'm here to tell you that there's a bunch of miners up there fixing to pay a call on your prisoners."

"Planning a little necktie party, are they?" scoffed Cozens. "Well, let them come, if they must. I'm prepared for them." He patted the shotgun. "Not that I really want to use this thing."

"Well, if I can help, Sheriff, I'm at your service."

"I certainly appreciate the offer, Mr. Creed. Are you competent with weapons?"

"I survived three and a half years in the Confederate cavalry, Sheriff. Does that say anything for me?"

"I wouldn't know, Mr. Creed. I didn't fight in the war myself. I had enough to do right here in Gilpin County keeping law and order."

"From what I've heard about these parts, I'd say that was a pretty tall order, sir."

"It has had its moments. Take this bunch we brought in this morning. We chased them for six days until we caught up with them in the Snowy Range. They tried shooting it out with me and my boys, but after we'd killed three of them, the other four threw up their hands and surrendered."

"Well, it would be a shame to have those men lynched, considering how much trouble you went to to bring them in for a fair trial and all."

"Yes, it would at that," said Cozens. "Is that your only interest in all this, Mr. Creed?"

"Not exactly, Sheriff. I heard that one of your prisoners is a Texan. Is that correct?"

"Yes, sir, it is."

"His name wouldn't be Marshall Quade, would it?"

"That isn't the name the prisoner gave when we caught him. Why do you ask?"

"I served with Marsh Quade in the war. We're from the same county back in Texas. His in-laws in Kentucky told me that he and his wife had come to Colorado to settle, and I thought I would look him up while I was here. When I heard that a Texan was among the outlaws that you had captured, I thought Marsh might have fallen into bad company."

"I don't know any Marshall Quade personally," said Cozens, "but I have heard the name before, although I can't rightly recollect exactly where I heard it at this particular minute. Do you think it possible that my prisoner could be this man that you're looking for, only using a false name?"

"He could be," said Creed, "but I'd have to see him before I could say for certain one way or the other."

Cozens nodded, thought for a second, then said, "Are you carrying a sidearm, Mr. Creed?"

"Yes, sir, I am." Creed opened his coat to expose the butt

of his Colt's. "I'll gladly surrender it to you, if that's what you're getting at, Sheriff."

"That's exactly my intention, Mr. Creed."

Creed dismounted, tied Nimbus to the rail, and stepped up to the edge of the jail landing. With the index finger and thumb of his left hand, he pulled the six-gun from his waistband and handed it over to Cozens. "I don't carry a knife on my person, Sheriff, in case you're interested."

Cozens hacked a laugh and said, "As a matter of fact, I was just gonna ask you that very question." He burped another chuckle. "Damned if you don't beat all. You don't read minds, do you, Mr. Creed?"

"No, sir, I don't. Let's just say that I've passed this way before."

The lawman turned serious. "Sure, I get your drift. Come on inside and have a look at this man I've got locked up in my jailhouse."

Cozens stepped aside and allowed Creed to precede him into the jail. A half-dozen deputies armed with Sharps rifles loitered in the ten-by-eighteen office. They eyed Creed suspiciously when he entered the room.

"Easy, boys," said Cozens. "This is Mr. Creed. He's come to have a look at our Texan to see if he's a friend of his from back home." He pointed to a plank door in the back wall. "The lock-up is straight through there, Mr. Creed. After you, sir." Over his shoulder, he said, "You boys go out front and keep an eye out for trouble. Mr. Creed says the miners up in Nevadaville are getting up a necktie party for our friends."

As all but one deputy followed the sheriff's orders, Creed opened the door and stepped into a long hall that led to a rear exit. To each side of the corridor were the cells, three to the left and three to the right. Each one had a wooden door with a small, barred window in it.

"He's in the middle cell on the right," said Cozens.

Creed peeked through the bars at a man sitting on the lower bunk. He studied the narrow, dirty, unshaven face staring back at him, then announced, "That's not Marshall Quade, Sheriff."

"You're certain about that, Mr. Creed?"

"Positive. The Marshall Quade I knew was a big-boned fellow with sandy hair and a heavy beard." He chuckled and added, "In fact his beard was so heavy that even after shaving himself clean he looked like he needed a shave. No, Sheriff, that man in there is not Marshall Quade."

"I didn't think so, Mr. Creed, but it never hurts to double-check. He says his name is David Jenkins."

"I knew a David Jenkins once. He was a lying, thieving lawyer, but this isn't him. The Jenkins I knew used the law to do his stealing. No way would he have the backbone to use a gun to rob an honest man."

"I know the kind of varmint you speak of, Mr. Creed," said Cozens. "Snakes in the grass is what they are. They'll put the bite on you when you ain't looking and without a lick of warning."

"That's David Jenkins all right," said Creed.

They returned to the office where a single deputy remained on duty.

"This Marshall Quade you spoke of," said Cozens, "I know I've heard of him somewhere."

"I heard of him," said the deputy standing next to a window and leaning against the wall. The man was gaunt, mangy, and clad in buckskin. He spat tobacco juice in the brass spittoon next to the jailer's desk.

"Mr. Creed, this is Charley Utter," said Cozens. "Charley did the scouting for me on this recent manhunt. You say you know this Marshall Quade, Charley?"

Utter squinted at Creed with a wary eye. "What's your interest in Quade, Mr. Creed?"

Creed figured Utter to be one of the fabled mountain men that he'd heard tales about as a boy. Like wild Indians, they were supposed to possess a keen sense of honesty, being truthful and forthright themselves and expecting the same from others who came in contact with them. To be sure, they told whoppers for entertainment, but when the griz stood on his hind legs, they spoke straight and true. To do otherwise could mean the worst. With this basic knowledge in mind, Creed opted to level with Utter.

"Marshall Quade is from the same part of Texas that I hail from, Mr. Utter," said Creed. "We rode together for a while during the war. After the war, he got mixed up in some bad business in Mississippi, and an innocent man got blamed for it. I'm hoping to find Marsh and convince him to come back to Texas to help me clear up this matter."

"You a lawman?" asked Utter.

"No, sir."

"Why do you want him to go to Texas?" asked Cozens. "I thought you said this bad business happened in Mississippi."

"Well, Texas might not be the exact place, Sheriff. We might have to go to New Orleans or even Washington City."

"Why there?" asked Cozens.

"It's an Army matter, ain't it?" said Utter.

"That's right," said Creed.

"An Army matter?" queried Cozens. "I thought you said you served in the Confederate cavalry during the war."

"I did say that, Sheriff."

"Then what has the Army got to do with this?" asked the lawman.

As quickly and as succinctly as possible, Creed told the story of how Jack Blackburn led a raid on an Army wagon train in Mississippi the month after the war ended and how Blackburn and the others who were captured later, including

Quade, put the blame on an innocent man, Clete Slater, and how Slater was tried by a military court, convicted, and sentenced to hang, only to escape. "And now I'm trying to help Slater clear his name," he said in conclusion.

"No good," said Utter. He aimed an accusing glare at Creed. "You're him, ain't you?"

Without batting an eyelash, Creed returned Utter's look and said, "Yes, I am."

Cozens was astounded. "You're wanted by the Army?"

Creed shifted his view to the sheriff and said evenly, "That's right, I am."

Without thinking, Cozens leveled his shotgun at Creed. "Then I'm arresting you, Mr. Creed . . . or whatever your name is."

"Aw, Billy, put that gun away," said Utter, "and start using some good sense here. Do you think this man would tell us all that if he was guilty? Think about it, Billy."

Cozens stared at Utter for a few seconds, then he shifted his gaze back to Creed. He lowered the shotgun and said, "I see what Charley's getting at now. I guess you wouldn't tell us all that business if you were truly guilty, Mr. Creed."

"Of course, he wouldn't," said Utter. "Like I said, I know Marshall Quade. He's been working as a bouncer at Schonecker & Mack's Billiard Parlor on Main Street most of the summer."

"That's where I heard of him," said Cozens.

"Schonecker & Mack's Billiard Parlor on Main Street?" queried Creed.

"That's right," said Utter, "but he ain't there now. He went back to Denver the other day to see his wife. Said he was lonely." He snickered. "I told him he could pay two dollars for one of the girls up in Nevadaville and save himself the stagecoach fare between here and Denver. He told me to go to hell. Said his woman would show a lot more appreciation for his talents than some bawdy bitch." A distant remembrance shaded his face. "Thinking back to the time I had me a Ute squaw and I'd be gone for days checking my trap lines and how she'd act when I'd come home . . . Yep, I think I can see what he was talking about now."

"Do you know where they live in Denver?" asked Creed.

"That's something I can't tell you, friend," said Utter. "All I know is he said he'd be back by Saturday night. That's when things get busiest around these parts. Ain't it so, Billy?"

"Sure is, Charley."

"What day is this?" asked Creed.

"What day is it?" repeated Cozens.

"I've been up in the mountains for a while," said Creed, "and I sort of lost track of time."

"It's Tuesday," said Cozens.

"Well, I don't think I want to wait for Quade to come back here Saturday. I think I'll ride down to Denver and look for him there."

"Well, you might as well wait and go in the morning," said Cozens. "It's almost sundown. Besides, I'd like you to be around here if those fellows from Nevadaville decide to come down here and lynch my prisoners." He held Creed's six-gun out to him. "How about it, Mr. Creed?"

Two little voices took up an argument in Creed's conscience. One said that he'd best be moving on, that this wasn't really any of his affair, that he had business of his own to tend to. The other told him to stay put and help out here because he believed every man deserved a fair and honest trial, guilty or not, especially because he'd been deprived of justice himself. Go, said one. Stay, said the other.

"Is it legal to deputize a convicted man, Sheriff?" asked Creed as he accepted the Colt's from the lawman.

Cozens snorted a laugh and said, "Hell, this is my county. I can do whatever I want."

15

Just as they'd said they should, the angry miners from Nevadaville marched down the gulch road to Central City to confront Sheriff Billy Cozens. The lynch mob planned to hold a come-as-you-are necktie party, and they needed some outlaws to be their guests of honor. They presented themselves outside the county jail in the evening twilight, demanding that Cozens release his prisoners to them. Jack Burch, Bill Rust, and Jake Williams, the brother of the murdered man and a robbery victim himself, vanguarded the procession of men gone mad, with blood in their eyes and revenge in their hearts.

Word that a lynch mob was coming down the road from Nevadaville circulated through the gulch as fast as news of a gold strike, and men from all walks of life in every town from Black Hawk to Russell Gulch dropped whatever they were doing and headed for the jail on Spring Street to witness the hanging—if there should be one. They stood everywhere, all trying to get close enough to hear and see everything that happened.

"Hand them over, Sheriff," said Burch, "and let us save the county attorney a lot of trouble trying this bunch."

Unarmed, coat open, hands on his hips, feet spread wide as he stood alone on the landing of the jail, Cozens smiled broadly and said, "And put the poor man out of work? Boys, where's your sense of decency? Ain't times around here tough enough as they are? Do we have to put another man out of work? I'll admit he's just a lawyer, but even lawyers have to eat."

"Cut the bullshit, Sheriff," said Burch. "We aim to hang those dirty thieving Rebs, and we aim to do it tonight. Now are you gonna hand them over or not?"

"Now you boys know I can't do that."

"Is that your final word on the subject, Sheriff?" asked Rust.

"I'm afraid it is, Bill."

Burch turned to the mob behind him. "All right, men, we'll have to go in after them." He turned back and took a step toward the jail.

The crowd surged forward.

Creed and Charley Utter, both armed with rifles, jumped through the front door of the jail. Each fired skyward, jacked another cartridge in the chamber, then took menacing aim at the mob's leaders.

"I'll kill the first man to step onto the landing," warned Utter.

"And I'll kill the second," said Creed.

The lynchmen halted.

"I've got five more men inside with shotguns," said Cozens. He smiled as he reached behind his back and produced his Colt's. "Just in case you get past the three of us."

"What's it gonna be, boys?" said Utter. "Do we start killing? Or are you gonna start showing the good sense the good Lord gave you when He put you on this earth?"

"You wouldn't shoot your friends, would you, Charley?" asked Rust.

"Ain't none of you my friends," said Utter. "Most of my friends are long since dead, and to tell you true, it wouldn't bother me none if I had to see some of them again up yonder right soon. Any of you boys interested in meeting a few of the old mountain men who was here and gone long before any of you was dry behind the ears yet?"

"You shouldn't be this way, Charley," said Rust.

"Who's that up there with Utter and the sheriff?" asked Jake Williams.

Only Burch and Rust knew Creed, but neither of them had noticed him in the fading light. Both leaned forward for a good look.

"It's that goddamn Texan!" swore Burch. "So you came down here to help your friends, did you, Reb?"

"I came down here to help the sheriff," said Creed.

"Lying sonofabitch!" shouted Burch. "He's one of them Rebs, Sheriff. He's mixed up with that bunch you got locked up inside the jail."

"Now you know that's not true, Jack Burch," said Cozens, "and if you don't stop trying to incite a riot here, I'll lock you up, too. In fact, if you boys don't break this up pretty damn quick, I'll start remembering faces and get me enough warrants to arrest every one of you for disturbing the peace and whatever else I can think of while you're resting up in one of my jail cells."

"Aw, you wouldn't do that, now would you, Sheriff?" said Rust.

"The hell I wouldn't! Now go on and git out of here before I start taking names!"

"You already know me," said Burch. "I'm Jack Burch, and I demand that justice be done this night. Those sonsabitches deserve to be hanged for killing John Williams, and we intend to do the deed, and we intend to do it tonight."

"Maybe they do deserve to be hanged," said Cozens, "but it ain't up to you to decide that, Jack Burch. Outlaws or not, those men have the right to a fair and honest trial."

Burch turned to the mob again. "We'll give the sonsabitches a trial, won't we, boys?"

A general murmur of agreement spilled out of the crowd.

"I'm talking about a trial in a court of law," said Cozens. "With lawyers and a judge and a jury."

"We don't need any goddamn lawyers to get in the way of justice, Sheriff," said Burch, "and every man here will be their judge and jury. Ain't that right, boys?"

More murmurs of agreement.

Before Cozens could raise his voice to silence the crowd again, Mary Cozens drove up the street in a buggy. The bystanders parted like the Red Sea to let her pass.

"Aw, hell!" swore Cozens under his breath. "What's she doing here?"

A hush fell over the crowd.

Mary reined in the horse pulling her buggy at the edge of the lynch mob where one of the men took hold of the animal's harness to hold it steady as Mary alit. She went around to the back of the conveyance, picked up a large wicker basket, put the handles over her arm, and turned toward the jail landing.

The lynchmen opened an aisle for her.

Mary walked placidly through the miners, her starched skirt rustling with every step. She stepped onto the boardwalk in front of her husband. "Mr. Cozens, I'm truly angry with you," she said loudly, her accent tinged with a bit of the brogue. She turned sideways to let the throng hear her better. "When you asked me to marry you, you promised that I'd never have to cook again for more than one man at a time for the rest of me days. So now I try to do a decent thing by bringing some food for you and your deputies and you go and invite the whole gulch to supper."

A roar of laughter rumbled from every throat in the crowd. Every throat except Burch's.

Seeing the sudden change in the crowd's mood and wishing to seize the moment, Utter stepped forward and said, "Don't go blaming Billy, Mrs. Cozens. It was Jack Burch there who's responsible for this gathering. I told him that you'd be bringing food and that he might like to join us for a bite, but he was to keep his mouth shut about it, what with everybody in these parts knowing your reputation as the finest cook in the gulch. I knew if word got out that every man that heard it would be wanting some. But, oh, no! Jack couldn't keep his big mouth shut, and look what happened, ma'am." He waved generously at the spectators.

Another roar of laughter. Except from Burch.

Shaking her finger at Rust, thinking him to be Burch, she said, "Just for that, Jack Burch—"

"He's Burch, Mrs. Cozens," interjected Rust, pointing at his friend. "I'm Bill Rust."

Without missing a beat, Mary said, "Well, it was an honest mistake. Your mouth looks to be as big as his."

Another roar of laughter. Except Burch.

"As I was saying, Jack Burch," she continued, "for inviting all these men without permission, there'll not be any pie for you for dessert. No, sir."

More laughter from everybody except Burch.

Mary turned on Utter. "And as for you, Charley Utter, just so's you'll learn a lesson here, you'll not get any pie for your dessert neither."

More laughter. Except Burch.

Turning serious now, Mary focused on the mob and said, "I know all of you were expecting to eat with the sheriff and his deputies and all, but I have to tell you that this basket ain't big enough to hold enough food to feed the whole lot of you. So if you don't mind, I'll be asking you to forgive me this time, and maybe some other time you can join the sheriff for supper. But please, let a woman know in good due the next time you all want to show up for a meal, so's I can prepare properly."

All roared. Not Burch.

"Now if you'll be excusing us," said Mary, "we'll be going inside to eat our supper. Good evening to you all."

"Now just wait a minute," said Burch. "I'm not budging from this spot until justice is served."

Having had his fill of Burch, Creed jumped down from the landing and said, "I think you've said enough, Mr. Burch." Without further ado, he slammed the stock of his rifle into Burch's jaw and knocked him into next week.

Silence fell over the crowd.

Creed looked up at Mary Cozens and said, "I'm sorry I had to do that, ma'am."

"It's all right, young sir," said Mary. "I wasn't serving any justice with the meal no how."

16

Only a glow of sunlight remained when Creed rode wearily into Denver Wednesday evening. He opted to register at the Colorado House and board Nimbus at the Elephant Corral.

The next morning he set out afoot for M. L. Rood's Gun Shop on F Street. Not that he figured he needed a new rifle to hunt Quade, but because he felt obligated to complete the deal that he'd made with Rood. First, he stopped at the First National Bank of Denver to make a small withdrawal.

"Good morning, Mr. Creed," said Rood with a friendly smile. "I was beginning to wonder if some terrible tragedy hadn't happened to you in the mountains and you might never return for your rifle."

"How did you know that I went to the mountains?"

"Your friend Ikard stopped by the Sunday that you left and told me that you'd departed town for a while, but that I was to hold your rifle for you, that you'd be back for it. I guess he knew what he was talking about."

Creed chuckled at the thought that Ikard was so wise to tend to this piece of unfinished business for him. "That sounds like Bose all right. Of course, you know he only did that because he wants that Henry of mine so bad."

"He said you'd say that."

Both men laughed.

"Did he tell you anything else, Mr. Rood?"

151

"As a matter of fact, he did. He said you could send the Henry to him care of Mr. Loving at Fort Sumner, New Mexico Territory. Does that make sense to you, Mr. Creed?"

"Yep, it does," said Creed, nodding. "Mr. Loving is taking the outfit back to New Mexico to meet his partner, Mr. Goodnight, who's bringing another herd up from Texas. They're planning to winter down there while they sell off the herd. I would guess that they'll be returning to Texas in the spring to round up another herd to bring back up this way next summer. It would only make good sense to do that, considering the shortage of beef in these parts."

"Yes, of course. Well, if you like, Mr. Creed, I can ship the Henry down to Fort Sumner for you. For a small fee, of course."

"Of course," said Creed. "I'll fetch it from my horse. One minute, sir." He went outside and retrieved the rifle. In a minute, he was back inside the gun shop. "Here you go, Mr. Rood." He handed the Henry to the gunsmith.

"And here you go, Mr. Creed." Rood presented the shiny new Winchester to Creed. "I hope you never have to use this weapon on a man, but if you do, it will never fail to shoot true."

"I hope I never have to find that out, Mr. Rood." Creed accepted the gun. "How much do I owe you?"

"That'll be thirty-eight dollars."

Creed never blinked at the price. He dug in his trouser coin pocket, pulled out two double eagles, and handed them to Rood. "Will the extra two dollars cover the cost of shipping my Henry to Fort Sumner?"

"That will cover my small fee. The shipping will be another ten dollars."

Creed took his last ten-dollar gold piece from his pocket and gave it to the gunsmith.

"I'll put the Henry on the next stage heading south," said

Rood. "It should arrive at Fort Sumner just about the same time as your friends."

"Very good," said Creed. "Now about another piece of business, Mr. Rood. I'm desirous of locating a fellow who served with me in the war, and I was told in Central City that his wife lives here in Denver."

"You were told this in Central City?"

"I know that sounds strange, but it seems the fellow—his name is Marshall Quade—it seems that he works at a billiards parlor in Central City, and his wife lives down here in Denver. Now I don't know why that is. I only know that's the situation with them. In the past, when I've looked for him, I've gone to the local post office to make inquiries about him, and in Nashville, I went to a newspaper office to start looking for him because I'd heard that he'd been in a bit of trouble and I thought they might have published the news. My hunch worked. The newspaper story told me where I might locate Quade's in-laws. I found them, and they told me that he and his wife came here."

"Have you tried the post office here?" asked Rood.

"No, I haven't. Denver isn't as large as Nashville, but I think it's too large for the postmaster to know everybody in town."

"That's most likely true, especially since so many people come and go here all the time. I hazard to guess that maybe half the people who reside here in Denver haven't been here more than a year. Maybe much less than that. When did these people come here, Mr. Creed?"

"Within this calendar year. I know they spent a short spell in Kentucky and another in Missouri before coming to Denver. I'd have to say that they arrived here in February or March at the latest."

"I see," said Rood. "Well, if I was a stranger here in Denver and I was looking for somebody, I'd still go to the office of

The Rocky Mountain News and ask Mr. Byers about the new city directory that he's publishing over there."

"A city directory?"

"Yes, sir. From what I've read in the *News*, it's gonna list every man in the city who owns a business or who works regularly, and that's supposed to include ladies who own businesses or who work regularly. If your man's wife lives here in the city, she just might be one of those working women that Mr. Byers will be listing in his directory. Even if she isn't, he'll have a list of boarding houses where she might be living. Either way, I'd start by asking about his directory, if I were you, Mr. Creed."

Creed nodded and said, "I think I'll do that, Mr. Rood. I thank you for the advice." He held up the Winchester and added, "And I thank you for this rifle, too."

"Thank you for the business, Mr. Creed, and good luck with your search for your friend."

They said farewell, and Creed left the gun shop for the offices of *The Rocky Mountain News* on Arapahoe Street west of Cherry Creek. Creed inquired about the new city directory, and a clerk told him that the directory wasn't completed yet, that it would be two or three more months before it was bound and ready for distribution.

"That's disappointing," said Creed. "I was hoping to use your directory to locate an old acquaintance who recently moved to this fair city."

"How recently?" asked the clerk, a short, bearded fellow wearing ink-stained sleeve garters and spectacles.

"Last spring."

"Well, if he works here in Denver, we'll have him in the directory."

"That's just it," said Creed. "He works in Central City, and his wife resides here in Denver."

"That's nothing unusual in these parts, Mister. Lots of men

work up in the mountains during the summer months and live down here in the winter. It gets pretty darn cold up there, and it snows to beat the band up there, too. Sometimes in the winter the snow gets so bad up in the mountains that we'll go two or three weeks without any news of Central City or the other towns up that way. It's only smart to live down here in the winter."

"I see," said Creed. "So where would you suggest I start looking for my friend's wife here in Denver?"

"Just a minute," said the clerk. He went to the back of the room to a stack of printed sheets, took the top page, and returned to the desk. "This is a list of hotels and boarding houses here in Denver. I'd start looking for your friend's wife at one of these. If she's not living at one of them, then she probably has employment in one of the shops on Blake or Larimer Streets and has a room or apartment over the store. You'll find that most of the employed ladies in Denver work in that vicinity. Blake and Larimer from E to G Street. If she isn't working over there, then I'd ask around with the clergymen, if she's a church-going woman, that is. That's how I'd go about it, if I were you, Mister."

"Sounds like good advice, sir," said Creed. He tipped his hat and bade the man farewell, taking the directory page with him.

Since he was already west of Cherry Creek, Creed started with the hotels and boarding houses on that side of town. The Tremont House, The California House, The Mansion House, Bell's Hotel, The Missouri House, The Atchison House, Devor's Corner, The Carter House, Bennett's Hotel, Rehfus boarding house, The Denver House, Stark & Co., and The Files House. The only place on the list that he passed over was The Firemen's Home. After lunching at the Colorado House, he began making inquiries at the hotels and boarding houses east of the creek. He worked his way northeast along

Blake Street to G Street, visiting The German House, Mrs. Karns's boarding house, The Rocky Mountain House, and The Planters' House. Turning down G Street to Larimer, he called at The Pacific House.

"Yes," said George Noble, one of the two proprietors, who was clerking at the front desk, "Mrs. Quade does reside here, but she isn't in right now." The owner was a thin, wiry man with a full, black mustache, pale complexion, balding pate, and ordinary blue eyes.

"Do you know when she'll be returning?" asked Creed.

"She's at her place of employment right now," said Noble, "and she won't be returning here until after six o'clock."

Creed noted that the time on the lobby clock was 3:16. He would have to wait three hours for her. Damn! he thought. So close and yet so far. But wait. What about Quade? "I was told in Central City that Mr. Quade had come down to Denver to visit his wife this week. Would he be here?"

"Yes, I do believe Mr. Quade was here this week, now that you mention it, although I can't recall seeing him today. But that's nothing unusual. He often sleeps most of the day while he's here. I understand he works the night shift at some mine near Central City."

Bouncer at a billiards parlor? thought Creed. Yes, he probably does work the night shift. "Do you think he's sleeping in their room right now?" asked Creed.

"That's hard to say, sir, but easy enough to find out. Just one minute, and I'll go check." Noble came from behind the desk and went upstairs. He returned in a few minutes to report, "I'm sorry, but he's not there."

"You're sure of that?"

"Positive. He puts a little note on the door asking visitors to be quiet because he's sleeping. There was no note on the door, and when I knocked, there was no answer. He's not there."

"I see," said Creed with disappointment. "You wouldn't happen to know where Mrs. Quade is employed, would you?"

"Yes, I do," said Noble. "She works at Mrs. Ermerins's millinery shop down the street between E and F. You can't miss it."

"Thank you, sir," said Creed. He tipped his hat and left the hotel. He walked along the boardwalk toward F Street and saw two other ladies' hat stores, one belonging to a Mrs. Palmer and the other owned by Mrs. Williams, the lady that he'd met after church on his previous visit to Denver. Thinking of her rang up the memory of Mattie Whittaker again, and guilt twisted his conscience.

What did I do to that girl? he asked himself. I loved her, and I lay with her, and I left her to pay the price for that one night of passion. But how was I to know that she would have my child? He grimaced and chastised himself. That was a stupid question, son. What other consequence of laying with a woman is there? Poor Mattie! What did I do to you?

Creed glanced up at the windows in the second story of Mrs. Williams's store. Both were open, and in one, he saw the little girl who had been with Mrs. Williams at the church. He made eye contact with her, and he was delighted to see her face burst into a beautiful smile. He stopped and waved at her, and she returned the greeting eagerly. He couldn't hear her, but he was certain that she was calling his name. He called back to her, "Hello, Cletia!"

The girl turned away from the window, "Mommy, Mommy, it's him! Come and see! It's him, Mommy! It's him. The man who told me about the knight and the princess. It's him, Mommy."

Creed couldn't see all of the person beside Cletia; only her dress from the neckline down; her face was hidden behind the glass which reflected the afternoon sunlight. He assumed it was the child's mother. He was right.

"That's him, Mommy," said Cletia, pointing at Creed standing on the boardwalk across Larimer Street.

"Yes, Cletia, I see," said the mother softly.

"Isn't he handsome, Mommy?"

"Yes, Cletia, he is."

Mrs. Williams entered the room.

"Auntie, it's him," said Cletia. "The handsome man from church who told me about the knight and the princess."

Mrs. Williams stepped over to the window and gazed down at Creed. "So it is," she said. She turned to Cletia's mother and saw that she was crying. "Oh, Mattie, not another one?"

Mattie Whittaker didn't answer.

"What's wrong, Mommy?" asked Cletia.

"Nothing, darling," said Mrs. Williams. "Your mother is all right." She glanced back at Creed. "It's only the dust from the street that makes her eyes tear that way." She looked down at Cletia and added, "Why don't you go to the kitchen and have a cookie, Cletia? I put three of them on a plate on the table for us."

"Oh, goodie, a cookie!" shrieked the child as she raced across the room toward the kitchen.

"Mattie, you've got to stop this," said Mrs. Williams. "He isn't the one either."

"But he looked so much like him, Clara."

"Yes, dear, I know," said Mrs. Williams as she put an arm around Mattie's shoulders and guided her toward the bedroom that she shared with her daughter. "Come and lie down now, and put him out of your mind."

"I can't, Clara. Not now that I know he's alive."

"Yes, dear, I know," said Mrs. Williams. Under her breath, she cursed Mattie's mother for writing Mattie that Cletus Slater had called on the Whittakers last winter. All she did was raise Mattie's hopes up that he would come back to her. Damn that man!

Creed saw the second lady join the first at the window, but he thought little of it as Cletia vanished from sight and was soon followed by the women. That lady reminds me so much of Mattie, he thought. I ought to go look for Mattie and do the right thing by her. Damn, son! Who are you kidding? You can't do anything right by anybody until you clear your name.

With that thought in mind, Creed continued along the boardwalk to Mrs. Ermerins's millinery shop in the next block. He stopped at the door as it occurred to him that he was a man entering a store for ladies. To hell with that notion, he told himself. He opened the door and stepped inside. Coming from the bright sunlight of the street into the dimness of the shop caused Creed to blink rapidly in an attempt to adjust his vision.

"May I help you, sir?"

Creed knew the voice to be that of a woman in her prime, although he still couldn't make out her face exactly to confirm the suspicion. "Uh, yes, ma'am," he stuttered. He blinked some more and focused on the fiery red-haired lady's sapphire eyes. "I'm looking for Mrs. Marshall Quade. You wouldn't be her, would you?"

In her thirties, slightly plump, an attractive blush coloring her cheeks, the woman blurted out, "I wish I was, but, alas, I'm not." Realizing how that must have sounded to him, she forced a giggle and muttered, "Oh, excuse me. I meant that I'm not Sal, uh, Mrs. Quade."

"Is she here?" asked Creed.

"I'm Sal Quade," said a younger voice from the back of the store.

Creed shifted his view to see Sal Quade walking toward him. She resembled her mother back in Tennessee: auburn hair, aqualine nose, eyes the color of hazelnuts, thin, fair complexion, and pretty. Very pretty. Too pretty for Marsh Quade,

Creed thought with his hormones instead of his head.

"Who are you?" she asked.

The Texan removed his hat, cleared his throat, and said, "Slate Creed, Mrs. Quade."

"Do I know you?"

"I wish I did," said the first lady. Embarrassed again, she said, "Oh, excuse me for butting in." She held out her hand. "I'm Bertha Ermerins."

Creed took her hand in his, smiled, and said, "How do you do, Mrs. Ermerins?"

"Much better now that I've seen you," she said. She gasped and covered her mouth with her free hand for a second before muttering, "Oh my! The things I say sometimes!"

"I'm flattered, Mrs. Ermerins."

"Aren't you nice to say that now?"

"You still haven't answered my question, Mr. Creed," said Sal. "Do I know you?"

"No, ma'am, I don't believe you do," said Creed, "but your husband does."

"Marsh knows you?"

"Yes, ma'am. We served together during the war."

"Then you must be from Texas. Yes, of course, you are." She paused to peruse Creed's face. "You're the man that my mother wrote me about, aren't you? Yes, you are. You're Clete Slater, aren't you?"

"As a matter of fact, I am, or at least I was until the Army convicted me of your husband's crime."

"Oh, a convict!" gasped Bertha.

"And so you've come looking to kill him for that?" said Sal, ignoring Bertha's remark.

"No, I don't want to kill him, although I probably should. No, Mrs. Quade, I don't want to kill Marsh."

"Then what do you want with him?"

"I want to take him back to Texas to tell the truth about

who was on that raid in Mississippi and help me clear my name."

"Now why would he want to do that?"

"Because if he doesn't come back to Texas with me, I will kill him."

"And where will that get you?"

"No place, but at least I'll have the satisfaction of knowing that one of the men who blamed me for their crime isn't living free any more."

Sal shook her head and said, "Sorry, Mr. Creed. Marsh told me about you. You're too honorable to kill a man in cold blood."

"I'm not the same man that Marshall Quade knew during the war, ma'am."

She studied him for a second, then said, "Yes, I can see that. You appear to be more like the man my mother wrote me about. That man wouldn't take anything lying down." Her head bobbed as a certain lascivious gleam came into her eyes. "No, you're nothing like the man Marsh told me about. You might kill him at that."

"I'd rather it didn't come to that, ma'am."

"I suppose I wouldn't want it to come to that either," said Sal. "Marsh isn't so bad. At least he got me out of Wrencoe."

"And now you're here," said Creed. "So would you mind telling me where I might find Marsh?"

"Sure, I'll tell you," said Sal. "If I don't, Bertha will. Won't you Bertha?"

"I . . . I . . ."

"Sure, she would," said Sal. "Well, he's on his way to Central City right this minute, Mr. Creed. He left Denver on the morning stagecoach."

17

A day late and a dollar short. Damn! How that old cliché seemed to haunt Creed.

The hour was too late for him to start out for Central City that Thursday. Just as well. He had one more piece of business in Denver that needed his attention before he left the city.

The Chicago Saloon was a much quieter place in the middle of the week than it was on the Saturday night that Creed had last stopped in. To be sure, it had its fair share of customers lined up at the bar, and Bob Stockton still sat on his stool guarding the gaming room in the back. One thing it didn't have was Jimmy Stockton lounging around waiting for trouble to come his way. All and all, the Chicago wasn't that bad a place under these conditions.

Or so Creed felt when he entered the establishment that evening looking for Hannah. When he didn't see her straight out, he walked carefully up to Bob Stockton, aware of the clear fact that the guard held a loaded shotgun in his hands and possibly a grudge in his heart, both of which could be used against Creed. "Good evening, Mr. Stockton," said the Texan, giving the guard a friendly nod.

"I thought we'd seen the last of you around here," said Stockton with a touch of annoyance. "What brings you back to the Chicago?"

"I'm looking for the serving girl who was here the last time I was in this place."

"You mean Juanita?"

"Yes, Juanita," said Creed, not giving any hint that he knew her by her real name. "Is she around?"

"Business is slow so Mr. Morton gave her the night off. She's probably upstairs in her room."

"Would it be all right if I went up to see her?"

"I don't suppose it would hurt anything, as long as you got the price for her time."

Creed frowned. He'd forgotten that Hannah served up more than drinks at this place. "Yes, I've got the money," he said evenly.

"Well, you know where her room is. Go on up."

Creed climbed the stairs and walked down the hall to Hannah's door. He knocked twice.

"*¿Quién es?*" Hannah called from within.

"It's me, Hannah. Slate Creed."

The door opened, and Hannah reached out, grabbed Creed by the arm, and pulled him inside. "You shouldn't call me that around here, Clete," she said. "They still think I'm a Mexican."

"You can't fool them forever, Hannah. Sooner or later, they'll find out that you were once a slave, and—"

"Don't you mean they'll find out that I'm a nigger?" she interjected bitterly.

Creed heaved a sigh, looked Hannah straight in the eye, and said, "No, Hannah, I don't mean that at all."

The look on Creed's face unsettled her a bit, but it wasn't enough to make her back off. "Sure, you do. Mammy was right. She told me that no matter what that I'd always be a nigger to you white folks. That I'd always be Dent's nigger whore."

Creed's emotions erupted. Pain and anger fought a desper-

ate battle within his soul. His temper exploded. He grabbed
her by the shoulders, shook her violently, and through gritted
teeth, he hissed, "Don't say that, Hannah. Don't ever say
that again. You're not Dent's nigger anything. You're not
a nigger. You're Hannah Slater. You're my brother's widow . . . whether what you said the last time is true or not."
Tears welled up in his eyes. He saw fright in her face. It
hurt him. "You're . . . you're my . . . my sister . . . and . . .
that's . . . all . . . there . . . is . . . to it . . . Hannah." He shook
her once more, then he pulled her hard against him, held her
close, and cried in her ear, "You're my sister, Hannah. My
sister, do you hear?"

"Your sister?" she gasped in his ear. "Do you mean it,
Clete? Your sister?"

"Yes, Hannah. You're my sister, and that baby . . . that
beautiful baby boy . . . he's my nephew."

Hannah threw her arms around Creed, buried her face in
his chest, and bawled, "Oh, Clete, Clete, Clete. I miss him
so much. I miss my Dent. I miss my Dent so much. I loved
my Dent so much, Clete, and they killed him. They killed my
Dent. I loved him so much, Clete. I loved him so much."

"I know, Hannah. I know. I loved him, too."

They cried together. For several minutes until Little Dent
interrupted them with his own cry.

Creed released Hannah, concerned for the crying child.

Hannah sniffled, wiped her eyes, picked up the infant, and
rocked him in her arms. "It's all right, Little Dent," she cooed
to the babe, a smile upon her lips. "It's all right."

Creed came close to her. "Could I hold him?" he asked
hesitantly.

Hannah smiled at Creed and said, "Sure, you can." She
handed the child to him.

Little Dent cried out.

"It's all right, Little Breeches," said Creed. Tears came to his eyes again. He looked at Hannah. "That's what we used to call his father when he was small. Remember?"

No, she couldn't remember, but she wanted to. Too choked up by Creed's love for her child, she could only nod.

"Yes, it's all right, Little Breeches," said Creed softly, looking back at the babe. "It's just me. Your Uncle Clete." He smiled at Hannah. "Yes, it's your Uncle Clete. That sounds right, doesn't it, Hannah?"

"It surely do."

The babe quieted.

Creed heaved a sigh, blinked away the remaining tears, and smiled at the mother. "He's a beautiful child, Hannah. You and Dent did good work here."

"Thank you, Clete."

"But you can't raise him here, Hannah. This is no place to raise a boy."

"I know, but where else can I go? I don't know where my family went except someplace in Kansas, and I can't even find Kansas."

"He needs to grow up and become a man in a place where he won't have to worry about being mistreated because some of his people came from Africa."

Caution suddenly painted Hannah's features. Her mother's words came back to her. "You'll always be a nigger to white folks." How she hated those words! How she hated the truth in them!

"Is that right?" she sneered. "And where would that place be? The moon?"

"No, Texas."

"Texas? Back to Lavaca County? Not on your life."

"No, not Lavaca County. Parker County."

"Where's that?" she asked.

"It's where my mother and her husband live now."

Confusion washed across her face for a few seconds as

she tried to decipher his words and understand them. "Your mother and her husband?" she queried. "Are you saying I should take Little Dent and go live with them?"

"Yes, except I'll take you there myself. I wouldn't want you and Little Dent to be traveling alone."

Hannah took the baby from Creed and placed him in his cradle again. She heard her mother's voice speaking that same refrain: "You'll always be a nigger to white folks." She looked Creed in the eye and said, "And you think your mother will accept me as Dent's widow and Little Dent as her grandchild?"

Creed heaved a sigh and said, "I'd be lying if I knew for sure that she'd accept both of you."

"That's what I thought, Clete. Well, we ain't going to Texas to live with your mother and her husband."

"At least go there with me and see how Mama and Howard feel about it."

"No, I ain't gonna take the chance that they won't let us through the door."

"They'll take you in, Hannah. I can guarantee that. They need help around the house."

"Help around the house? Are you saying they need a house nigger?"

Creed's head drooped as he realized how that sounded now. "Damn!" he swore. "That's not what I meant at all."

"Then what did you mean, Clete?"

He shrugged and said, "I only meant that Mama and Howard need help with the ranch. If I can get things straight with my life again, I'm gonna marry Texada, and we're gonna live with my folks and help them with the ranch. I just thought that with you and Little Dent being family that you'd want to do the same thing."

Hannah studied his face for any guile, and when she couldn't find any, she said, "Your mother was always good to us back at

Glengarry, but I wonder if that was because Massuh Dougald made her that way, the same way he made you and Dent and Malinda treat us good."

"Grandpa Dougald didn't have to make us treat you and your family decently. For heaven's sake, Hannah, you were pretty much family then. Didn't we grow up together?"

"Yes, we did, but that was before the war. We darkies knew our place then because we was slaves. Now I don't know where our place is. As best as I can see so far, it ain't being part of no white family."

"Will you forget that black and white business? You're not all African, and I'm not all European."

Hannah frowned and queried, "European?"

"White," explained Creed. "It's like this, Hannah. White people came from Europe. Black people came from Africa. Red people—Indians—were already here. I'm as much an Indian as I am a European. And you? You're as much a European as you are an African. Isn't that so?"

"In whose eyes?"

"In your own."

"In my own?"

"Yes, your own. Look, Hannah. I'm just as proud of my Choctaw and Cherokee ancestors as I'm proud of my Scottish ancestors. You should be proud of your ancestors because they're Little Dent's ancestors, too, and if I have anything to say about it, he'll be proud of the Scotsmen, the Cherokees, and the Choctaws—"

"And the Africans?" interjected Hannah.

"Yes, and the Africans, too," said Creed firmly. "Every man and woman who had a part in making him what he is. Or what he will be."

"And what will that be, Clete?"

"He'll be a Slater." He laughed. "Do you know what, Hannah? It just came to me that if your marriage to Dent is legal and all, then Little Dent is the rightful owner of Glengarry." He laughed louder. "Wouldn't that be a kick in Markham's cavalry breeches?" He laughed again before turning serious again. "Never mind that now. We'll cross that bridge when we get to it. Right now, we've got to get you and Little Dent away from this place."

"Well, we ain't gonna go to Texas to live with your mother and her husband. Not until I know for sure that we'll be family and not house niggers."

"All right, Hannah, I won't take you to Texas. How about the Chickasaw Nation."

"The Chickasaw Nation?" she repeated, disbelieving her ears. "Go live with Indians? You are crazy, Clete Slater. I ain't gonna go live with no Indians. Not on your life."

"You're right, Hannah. Not on my life. On Little Dent's life." He set his jaw to let her know that he meant every word.

Hannah stared back—afraid, excited, happy, uncertain. What should I do? she asked herself. Her eyes drifted toward her son, Dent's son, Creed's nephew. Clete loves Little Dent, she thought, but what about me? Does he really love me as his sister?

Creed sensed that something was wrong. He saw her indecision, and his heart reached out for her, then his hand touched her. "And your life, too, Hannah. I know some people who will accept you for *who* you are, not *what* you are. Do you understand?"

"Do you mean that it won't make no difference to them that I was once a slave and Little Dent is the son of a slave?"

"That's right. These are good people. They're missionaries that I met when I was crossing the Nations last spring. They have a mission in a place called Cherokee Town in the Chickasaw Nation. The best thing I can say about these people is they're colorblind."

"Colorblind?" she queried. Then it struck her what he meant by that.

"Yes, colorblind."

"And you say they live in the Chickasaw Nation? Are they Indians?"

"No, they're Northerners, and they've got a boy living with them named Little Bee Doak who's got mixed blood in him just the same as Little Dent here. They're teaching him to read and write and cipher numbers, and they're giving him religion, too. They could do the same for you and Little Dent, Hannah."

"Teach me to read and write and cipher numbers?"

"That's right, and Little Dent, too, when he's old enough to learn."

Hannah thought about it for a second more, then said, "All right, we'll go to the Chickasaw Nation with you."

Creed embraced her and kissed her cheek. "You'll see, Hannah. This is the right thing to do."

"When do we leave?"

He frowned. "Not yet. I've got that other business to tend to first." He explained what that was, finishing with, "I should be back here early next week. You get your things together and be ready to leave. In the meantime, I'll start thinking about how we'll get there. You just be ready to go when I get back."

"I'll be ready," said Hannah, although she didn't really believe that he would come back.

18

The stagecoach from Denver took a full, dry summer day to make the trip to Central City, and two days in winter—if no snow fell and the road was fairly free from mud. It could make such good time because the driver changed teams twice along the way. A man on a horse couldn't push that hard. Not going up the mountain. Not even under perfect conditions, such as those Creed had when he took all of Friday and most of Saturday to return to Central City.

Much to his surprise, Sheriff Cozens was waiting for Creed on the boardwalk outside Schonecker & Mack's gaming business. "Welcome back to Central City, Mr. Creed."

Creed alit and tied Nimbus to the hitching post. "Thank you, Sheriff. It's good to see you again."

"Thank you, sir."

"How are your prisoners doing?"

Cozens chuckled and said, "They're nervous, but they're safe and under close guard in the jail. Thank you again for helping me protect them the other night."

"You're welcome, Sheriff." He nodded at the entrance. "Are you going in there?"

"No, and I don't think you should either." Cozens blocked Creed's path to the door of the billiards parlor. "I'll get right to the point here, Mr. Creed. I know you didn't catch up with

Marshall Quade in Denver. I know because he came back here Thursday night, and he didn't say nothing about meeting up with you down below. And since you're back here, it means you're still looking for him. Am I right?"

"Right as rain, Sheriff." A lamp flickered in Creed's head. "Wait a minute. You didn't just happen to be here when I rode up. You've been waiting for me, haven't you, Sheriff?"

Cozens grinned sheepishly and said, "Yes, sir, I have."

"Then Quade knows I'm coming for him, doesn't he?"

"I'm afraid he does."

"And you expect there will be trouble if I go in there after him?"

Cozens nodded grimly. "If it was just you and Quade in there, I wouldn't be too concerned about anything. You got to work this out between the two of you. That much is certain. But it's Saturday, Mr. Creed, and the saloons in the gulch are beginning to fill up with miners and teamsters and all sorts of rough characters who don't care how they spend their money as long as they get a good time for it. Do you know what I mean?"

"I've got an idea," said Creed.

"I ain't so sure you do. Let me put it this way. This ain't Denver. Up here, when two gents start in with each other, it's usually a signal for everybody to jump into the affray, and in the bargain, a gent is sure to lose his grubstake if he ain't careful."

Creed stared hard at the lawman and said, "I'm not worried about that, Sheriff. I'm no gentleman."

"No, sir, I guess you ain't," said Cozens, stroking his beard. He stepped aside to allow Creed entry to the gaming establishment, thinking, You're much more than that, Slate Creed, much more.

Creed entered Schonecker & Mack's.

Although the six o'clock whistle had blown only an hour before at the mills and mines, signaling the end of the work day and the work week, the joint was fairly crowded already. The billiards parlor was one very large room with a bar on the left side, six billiards tables evenly spaced down the middle, and drinking tables, chairs, and a three-step gallery to the right. Two white-aproned bartenders served customers at the rail, and two serving girls moved among the tables waiting on players and spectators. Stationed on high stools in the rear of the hall were the bouncers, four brawny gents all armed with revolvers. Counted among these rule enforcers was Marshall Quade who started glaring at Creed as soon as he entered the premises.

"That's him," said Quade to his associates.

Creed scanned the hall, and much to his chagrin, he recognized Jack Burch, Bill Rust, and Jake Williams playing at the next to last table with a fourth man who Creed didn't know. Carefully and cautiously, he tried weaving through the players and tables, hoping the Indiana men wouldn't see him and give him cause for grief. He failed.

"Well, if it ain't the Reb from Texas," said Burch, moving to intercept Creed. His face was still swollen where Creed had slugged him with the rifle butt.

"Leave him be, Jack," said Rust, grabbing his friend's arm. "He was only helping the sheriff the other day."

"Helping his Reb friends, you mean," said Burch.

Sheriff Cozens had followed Creed into the hall.

"Easy, Jack," said Williams, moving close to Burch. "Billy Cozens just came in. We don't need no more trouble with him now."

Creed came near them.

"Mr. Creed," said Rust in a friendly manner.

"Gents," said Creed, giving the trio a cursory nod of greeting. He passed by them and didn't look back. Finally, he stood in front of Quade's stool, looking up at his former comrade-in-arms. "Long time no see, Marsh," he said evenly.

"Maybe too long, Slater. Maybe not long enough." Although he tried not to show it, Quade was afraid.

Creed sensed the fear in Quade. He also noted the other three bouncers staring at him, each with a hand near his weapon. He'd faced odds like this before, but never at this close range. "Too long," he said with a smile, "for old friends like you and me."

"Cut the crap, Slater. We was never friends."

"We rode together in the war, Marsh. That counts for something, doesn't it?"

"Not with me, it don't."

"Well, it does with me. That's why I couldn't figure you boys doing what you did to me."

"Well, you figured wrong, Slater."

"All right, I figured wrong, but you boys still had no call to lay the blame on me for that raid in Mississippi."

Quade's brow furrowed as he said, "It was either us or you, and since you wasn't around, we figured it was best that it be you."

"Well, you boys figured wrong, Marsh. I don't take things like that lying down. You boys should have known that about me."

"Well, it's done, Slater, and nothing can change it."

"That's where you're wrong again, Marsh. It can be changed. You can set things right just by coming back to Texas with me and telling the Army the truth about who really led that raid. That's all you have to do, Marsh."

"That's all I have to do?"

"That's right," said Creed with a friendly smile.

"I don't think so, Slater."

Beginning to feel a little frustrated, Creed let his head droop a second before saying, "Look, Marsh. I'm in a real fix because of what you boys did. I'm just asking you to come back to Texas with me and tell the Army the truth about that raid. That's all, Marsh. I'm asking. No threats. Just asking. Come back to Texas with me and tell the Army the truth. That's all you have to do, Marsh."

"That ain't so simple as it sounds, Slater," said Quade nervously.

"Sure, it is. If it's the cost of going back home that's bothering you, well, I can take care of that. You can bring that pretty wife of yours, too."

"How do you know my wife is pretty?" demanded Quade, jealously suspicious of Creed.

"When I was looking for you down in Denver, I paid a call on her at the ladies' hat store where she works. She told me that you'd come back here already."

"I can believe that," said Quade sarcastically.

"It's the truth, Marsh, but she didn't tell me until I told her that I wasn't looking to kill you for the trouble that you boys caused me."

"You ain't thinking to kill me, Slater?"

"Why would I do that? I need you to tell the Army the truth. That's it, plain and simple."

"No, it ain't that simple, Slater."

"Why isn't it, Marsh?"

Quade studied Creed for a moment, then said firmly, "You really don't know, do you?"

"Know what?"

Quade glanced at his fellow bouncers and noted how intently they were listening to the conversation. He slipped off his stool and said in a low voice that only Creed could hear, "Let's go sit over at that table where we can talk more private, but let me warn you. If you're lying about not wanting to kill me and you start something, my friends here will settle your hash in no time at all."

"I'll keep that in mind," said Creed.

They walked over to a drinking table between two billiards tables and sat down. Creed scanned the room quickly and noticed that Sheriff Cozens was standing just inside the front door, watching them. He nodded politely at Cozens, then returned his attention to the business at hand.

Quade bent close to Creed and in a conspiratorial tone said, "Those other fellows are Yankees." He indicated the other bouncers. "They don't need to be listening to our little talk here."

"No, I guess not."

"Good. Now you tell me what you know about the raid, Slater, and then I'll tell you what I know."

"I don't know much more than the facts that you, Jasper Johnson, Dick Barth, Dick Spencer, Jonas Burr, and Jack Blackburn were in on it, that you all got caught by the Army, and that all of you swore that I led the raid."

"That's all you know?"

"I know you killed some Yankees in the raid, and that's why they want to hang me. I know all about how you got caught up in Tennessee and how you and the others turned chicken and pointed the finger at me. I know about you getting married to Miss Sidney Ann Linn Perkins and that you went to Kentucky, then Missouri before you settled here. I know that the others are probably back in Texas now."

Quade's head bobbed with Creed's words, and when it was his turn to speak, he said, "But you don't know about that Yankee sonofabitch who told us that we'd hang if we ever changed our stories?"

"What Yankee sonofabitch?" queried Creed, suspicious that Quade was only making excuses.

"His name was Peck. You remember him, don't you, Slater? Colonel Peck? That sonofabitch who gave us the oath and signed our paroles?"

Creed remembered Peck. The memory wasn't pleasant. "He didn't sign my parole," said Creed bitterly as he recalled that day the year before.

When the Union armies had all but ended the war by late March of '65, Captain Cletus Slater decided that the war in the East was lost. With a small detachment of fellow Texans following him, he headed west to join General Edmund Kirby Smith's trans-Mississippi command, dodging Union patrols at every turn; but before they could reach the Mississippi, General Lee surrendered to Grant at Appomattox. News of Lee's and General Johnston's subsequent surrender in North Carolina and General Taylor's surrender in Alabama caused Slater and his men to rethink their plan to join Kirby's army.

"The war is over for all practical purposes," said Slater. "This insignia on my collar doesn't mean a thing now. We're all civilians again, and every man has the right to do as he pleases. As for me, I'm riding into New Orleans to surrender. Anybody who wants to is welcome to ride with me."

"I say we keep on to Texas," said Jack Blackburn. "The war isn't over there."

"It will be by the time we get there," said Slater. He heaved a sigh and added, "Besides, I'm tired of fighting these damn Yankees. You can go on to Texas if you like and keep on fighting. I'm going to New Orleans to surrender. Who's with me?"

A majority voiced the same opinion as Slater. Quade, Blackburn, Burr, Spencer, Johnson, and Barth made up the minority. Seeing that their small contingent wouldn't have much chance to reach Texas safely, they decided to surrender with Slater and the others.

As he was leading them toward New Orleans, Slater spotted a Union patrol on the road outside the city. He raised a white flag and approached the Federals cautiously. He saluted the

Union officer and introduced himself.

"How do you do, Captain Slater? I am First Lieutenant Albert Danforth." He looked nervously past Slater at the Confederates who outnumbered his unit three to one. "It appears you have the advantage, Captain."

Slater glanced over his shoulder at his men, then, quite perplexed, he stared at Danforth. "Advantage?" In another second, he understood and laughed. "Oh, no, Lieutenant. I've come to surrender to you."

"You have?" muttered Danforth.

"Yes, sir." Slater drew his sabre and offered it hilt first to Danforth. "The war is over, Lieutenant. We just want to go home."

Danforth took the sword, then he returned it. "I accept your surrender, Captain, but what would you have me do with you and your men?"

Slater smiled and said, "I thought you could lead us safely into New Orleans. I'm not so sure that if we came across a bigger bunch of you Yanks that we wouldn't have to fight our way into the city."

Danforth laughed and said, "Yes, of course, Captain. Just have your men fall in behind mine, and I'll see that you reach New Orleans safely."

And he did.

Along the way to New Orleans, Danforth explained General Grant's surrender terms to General Lee and how General Canby was extending the same terms to all Rebels who surrendered to his command. "You can expect fair treatment under General Canby," he said. That was before they met up with Colonel Walter Peck.

Until the month before Slater's arrival in Louisiana, Colonel Peck commanded a regiment of prison guards at Rock Island, Illinois. Feeling that his last chance to see any action would be in a campaign against General Kirby's Confederate army in Texas, he requested a transfer to General Canby's army in Louisiana. Although it was granted, he was disappointed to discover that General Canby had decided against mounting an offensive in Texas, feeling it would be only a matter of time before Kirby followed the lead of the other Rebel generals and asked for terms. Until then, his army would sit tight in Louisiana. Peck was assigned command of the prisoner of war camp in New Orleans where Danforth led Slater and his men.

"What do we have here, Lieutenant?" asked Peck on their arrival.

"Prisoners, sir."

"Prisoners? These Rebs still have their weapons. How can they be your prisoners if they're armed?"

"They surrendered peacefully, sir, so I saw no reason to disarm them."

"No reason to disarm them? Lieutenant, are you mad? These bastards are Rebels. They're traitors to the Union. They're murderers and rapists. They should be summarily shot for what they've done to our country. Disarm these bloody bastards right this minute."

"Hold on there, Colonel," said Slater. "Lieutenant Danforth told us the terms of surrender, and—"

Peck interrupted, "And what terms were these, Reb?"

Slater recognized the tone. Smug sonofabitch, he thought. If we were still fighting, I'd shoot him in the knee right now and get his attention real quick.

He didn't shoot him. Instead, he spoke patiently and firmly to the Yankee colonel. "We keep our sidearms and our horses."

"The hell if you do!" snapped Peck. He reached for the reins to Slater's Appaloosa.

The horse reared up and brought a hoof down on Peck's left shoulder, driving the man to the ground with the sudden agony of a broken clavicle. When the stallion calmed down and was under Slater's control again, Peck screamed, "I'll have you shot, you sonofabitch!" He winced with pain. "You'll pay for this, Reb! If it's the last thing I ever do, I'll make you pay for this. I swear it." Then he fainted.

Like many Southerners, Slater and his men took the oath of allegiance to the Union with their fingers crossed, and they were given paroles in New Orleans that said they were now loyal citizens of the United States again. After handing over their shoulder weapons, Slater hung around the city for a spell, then he headed home for Texas, but some of the other men rode north for Tennessee for what they called "one last raid" in the vicinity of Nashville—meaning they planned to visit some girls they had known there when they were fighting in that area.

"Do you mean to tell me that Peck put you boys up to blaming me for the raid?"

"That's about the size of it, Slater."

Creed was furious, but he kept his anger inside him. "When do you get through working here, Marsh?"

"Why do you want to know that?"

"I want to know when I should come around to fetch you for the trip to Texas."

"The hell, you say. I ain't going back to Texas with you or anybody else for that matter."

Exasperated by Quade's attitude, Creed drew his Colt's to force the issue. "All right, Marsh. I guess we can leave now instead of waiting for you to finish the night."

"He's gone for his gun!" shouted Quade, pushing the table into Creed's gut and effectively preventing Creed from bringing the six-gun to bear.

The other three bouncers jumped down from their stools and went for their guns.

Sheriff Cozens drew his Colt's and yelled, "Hold on there!" He broke toward the rear of the hall.

Quade popped to his feet and pulled his revolver.

"It's the Reb!" yelled Burch. He pushed his playing partner out of his way and swung his billiards cue at the back of Creed's head.

Men shouted warnings. Shots rang out. Gunsmoke filled the room. More shots. More shouting. Pandemonium. Men running in every direction, looking for cover. Some made it. One didn't. The stranger playing billiards with Burch, Rust, and Williams lay dead on the floor.

Creed lay beside him. Bleeding. Unconscious.

19

"Let's string 'em up!"

Not exactly words that Creed wanted to hear, especially when they applied to him.

"Now hold on here!" shouted Sheriff Cozens. "I'm arresting these men for disturbing the peace and—"

"Disturbing the peace?" echoed Jack Burch. "One of those sonofabitching Rebs killed Frank Derby, and they gotta hang for it."

A roar of similar sentiments exploded in the hall, and Cozens tried to silence it.

Creed didn't understand what was happening around him, and he didn't care all that much just yet. For the moment, he wanted to reach for his head, specifically, the back of it where it felt like somebody had taken a tomahawk to his skull. He couldn't get his hands up that high, however, because both arms were being held in the firm grips of two of the bouncers, and when he moved they tightened their holds on him. His eyes opened, but they had trouble focusing. Damn! he thought. What's wrong here, son? He was sitting in a wing chair, that much he knew. And he was wet—not all over, just around the head and shoulders. Why am I wet? He heard Cozens shouting above the general din. What's that all about now? He looked up to see a fuzzy sheriff looming between him and an even fuzzier crowd. He blinked rapidly to clear his vision. It hurt, but he succeeded. Now if he could only clear the pain from his head.

"Now we don't know who shot Derby," said Cozens once he got the mob to quiet down enough to hear him again.

"It was one of the Rebs," shouted Burch.

"We don't know that for sure," countered Cozens.

"It don't make no difference which one of them did it," argued Burch. "One of them did it, and that makes them all guilty."

"Yeah!" shouted Rust. "They started this ruckus, and we're gonna finish it. I say we hang the bastards." He spun on a heel to face the crowd. "Somebody get a rope."

The cobwebs began clearing from Creed's brain. He focused on Cozens in front of him; the sheriff's back was to him. Lord, he's a big man, thought Creed. He turned his head to the right. Damn! that hurts! He did it anyway and saw the bouncer holding him; the man was scared shitless. He looked to his left. What the hell hit me? he wondered as he winced with the pain of movement. He saw the other bouncer holding him; also scared out of his wits.

"Yeah!" railed Burch. "Somebody get a rope. Get two ropes, and let's hang them together. Sonofabitching Rebs! And when we're done with these two, let's hang those bastards in the jail."

"Yeah! Yeah! Yeah!" chorused the mob.

Creed remembered now. He'd drawn his Colt's to scare Quade—Quade? Where's Quade? he asked himself. He tried to look around more, but he couldn't see Quade anywhere in front of him. He must be behind me. Where's the other bouncer? They're both behind me most likely.

He was right. Quade and the fourth bouncer stood behind Creed and their two co-workers, all four of them holding their revolvers at the ready, prepared to fire into the mob that filled the hall now.

Cozens fired into the ceiling, then leveled his Colt's at Jack Burch's forehead. "The next one is for you, Burch," he growled like a grizzly. "This is the second time in a week that you've tried to start a lynching. Well, I've had my fill of you, friend. One more word from you, and I'll send you to Hell."

Burch backed away. Silent. Frightened. He knew from the fire in Cozens's eyes that the sheriff wasn't bluffing. Not this time.

Others followed Burch's example.

"Now that's more like it," said Cozens. "Now I'm placing all five of these men under arrest, and I'm taking them to jail where they're gonna stay until I can determine who shot Frank Derby."

Creed saw the body on the billiards table. Who's that? he wondered. He blinked and tried to remember. The fourth man playing billiards with Burch and Rust and Williams? Yes, it must be him. I don't see him with them now. He's dead. Somebody killed the poor fellow. Damn! They think I did it.

"I didn't kill him!" shouted Creed without thinking.

"Shut up, Reb!" said the bouncer to his left.

"I didn't kill him!"

"Shut him up," said Quade.

The bouncer to Creed's right raised his revolver to hit Creed in the head again.

Cozens did an about-face and said, "Leave him be."

The bouncer held off.

"I didn't kill him, Sheriff. I didn't even shoot my gun."

"What's this?" sputtered Cozens.

"He's lying," said Quade.

"Where's his gun?" demanded Cozens.

The bouncer to Creed's left handed it to the sheriff.

Cozens checked the charges and caps. None spent. He sniffed the muzzle. No fresh odor of burnt gunpowder. He turned back to the crowd and announced, "This gun hasn't been fired. He's telling the truth. He didn't kill Derby."

Silence. Disbelief everywhere.

The sheriff turned back to the bouncers holding Creed and said, "Let him go." When they didn't move immediately, he repeated the order, and this time he was obeyed.

"That means the other Reb did it," said Burch.

Cozens spun around again and drew a bead on Burch's forehead. "I warned you, Burch."

Burch flinched. His eyes bulged. His jaw dropped. His knees buckled.

The crowd parted behind him.

Cozens fired over Burch's head and broke a bottle of Old Taos on the backbar.

Burch fainted.

"Get him out of here," said Cozens.

Rust and Williams picked up their friend and headed for the front door.

"The next man to interfere with the law won't be so lucky," said Cozens. He was believed. He turned to Quade and the other bouncers. "One of you killed Derby. Anybody willing to 'fess up?"

Quade's coworkers shifted their gazes from Cozens to him. He looked back at each of them, his face paling more by the second. He stumbled backward against the wall. "I didn't kill him," he blurted out. "I didn't kill him. I swear it. I didn't do it."

Creed saw what was happening here, and he didn't like it. Now that the sheriff had exonerated him, the mad dogs were ready to settle for Quade's life. That wouldn't do. He needed Quade alive and well to talk to somebody who could help him clear his name legally.

"Now just hold on here," said Creed. He pushed himself erect. It hurt, but he did it anyway.

"Stay out of this, Mr. Creed," said Cozens. "I'm arresting Quade for killing Frank Derby, and I'm taking him to jail until the judge decides whether he should stand trial or not. Do you understand me, Mr. Creed?"

"Sure, Sheriff, I understand."

"I didn't kill him," whined Quade.

"Just shut your mouth," said the bouncer closest to him. He lashed out a meaty paw and slugged Quade in the jaw, knocking him senseless long enough for the others to disarm him.

"That's enough, boys," said Cozens. "I'll take him to jail now." He turned to the crowd. "You men go about your business."

The crowd obeyed.

The sheriff handed Creed his gun. "Better put this away, Mr. Creed. You don't have any need for it here."

Creed took the gun, nodded, and said, "Sure thing, Sheriff."

The crowd parted again and let Cozens and his prisoner pass between them to the front door.

The bouncer that struck Quade handed Creed his hat and said, "Get out, Reb."

Creed didn't have to be told twice. He tried to don his hat, but his head hurt too much to pull it down tight. Besides that, he felt the gash in his scalp and the caked blood in his hair where Burch had hit him with the billiards cue. Better find a doctor, he thought, and get this tended to right away. He left the hall, hat in one hand, Colt's in the other.

Darkness covered the town. A few street lamps provided some light, enough for Creed to see Cozens and Quade walking along Main Street toward its intersection with Spring and Nevada Streets. Also enough for him to make out Rust,

Williams, and Burch across the street in front of the Rocky Mountain National Bank.

"I'm not through with you yet, Reb!" Burch shouted at him. "We still got a score to settle, and we'll see to your friends, too."

Creed told himself that this wasn't the time to shut Burch up once and for all. He needed a doctor. That had to come first. But where to find one? Cozens would know. He untied Nimbus from the hitching post and hurried on foot to catch up with the sheriff and his prisoner.

Cozens heard Creed coming up fast behind him in the dark. He stopped and spun around, Colt's ready to kill. "Come any closer and I'll shoot," he warned.

"It's only me, Sheriff. Slate Creed."

"Come ahead, Mr. Creed, if you must, but I told you that it won't do you any good. I'm taking Quade to jail, and that's all there is to that."

Creed came close to Cozens. "Sheriff, I was hit in the head in that fracas back there. I need a doctor to look at my injury."

"That's right. You were bleeding pretty bad for a while. I thought Burch had staved in your skull permanent when I first saw you lying there on the floor, but you were still breathing and that bucket of water brought you around quick enough."

"I don't recollect any of that, Sheriff."

"No, I guess not. Burch hit you pretty hard with that cuestick. Better come along to the jail with me for now, and I'll send one of the boys out to find a doctor for you."

"Sounds like a fair idea," said Creed.

They went on to the jail, where Cozens locked Quade in the last vacant cell. Then he sent the jailor on duty to find a doctor for Creed and to round up the other deputies.

"Are you expecting more trouble?" asked Creed.

"I don't think we've heard the last we're gonna hear from Jack Burch and those miners up to Nevadaville. This is the second friend of theirs to be killed in the last two weeks. They want somebody to hang for those killings, and I don't think they're willing to wait for a jury to find these boys guilty and a judge to sentence them, all legal and proper. This is Saturday night, and every man in town is filling his belly with beer or whiskey. Am I expecting trouble, Mr. Creed? You bet."

"Have you thought about moving your prisoners to a safer place, Sheriff?"

"Sure I have. As soon as all my deputies report in, that's exactly what I plan to do. And as soon as everybody gets back to work on Monday morning and things cool off around here, I'll bring them back and let the law take its course."

The deputy returned with a doctor, and the physician tended to Creed's scalp laceration. He cleaned it with an alcohol and iodine solution that burned like the fires of Hell, then he poured laudunum on it to numb the area before sewing up the wound with three stitches. He warned Creed that the stitches would begin to itch the next day and that he wasn't to scratch them. "You leave them alone, no matter what, or you'll get a poison in there that I won't be able to get out."

Charley Utter showed up at the jail as the doctor was leaving. He nodded at Creed and said, "Heard about Jack Burch smashing your gourd with a billiards cue. Just like that yellow shittin' coward to hit a man from behind." He turned to Cozens. "Burch is up in Nevadaville right now, stirring up the miners at Maxwell's to come down here and lynch every one of your prisoners, Billy. It wouldn't surprise me none if they waited a few more hours to drink their fill of courage and stupidity before they come down here, though. You gonna stick around and help us again, Mr. Creed?"

"No, Mr. Creed ain't gonna help us this time, Charley," said Cozens. "He's leaving town immediately."

"I am?"

"Yes, sir, you are."

"Why would I want to do that, Sheriff?"

"To save your own hide. If I know Burch at all, I know he won't be satisfied just to hang this bunch I've got locked up in here. That dumb sonofabitch wants you just as dead as he wants these boys. And I've seen enough of you to figure that you won't let him do anything without you putting up one hell of a good fight, and if you do, Burch and probably four of his friends will be filling graves come Monday morning. Am I right, Mr. Creed?"

"That's about the size of it, Sheriff. I wouldn't let them string me up without sending a few of them through the Pearly Gates ahead of me."

"That's what I thought," said Cozens. "So why don't you get your horse and ride on out of town. Go over to Black Hawk for the night, and tomorrow you can leave the gulch for good."

"That sounds like an order, Sheriff."

"If that's what it takes to keep you and a handful of our citizens alive, then that's what it is, Mr. Creed."

Creed nodded and said, "Well, thank you, Sheriff, for saving my life back at the billiards hall. I'll never forget that."

"You can thank me by getting out of town, Mr. Creed."

"Consider me gone."

20

What was it Ouray said? Creed asked himself. "Ouray will be at Pedro's when you need him. Whenever that time will be, Ouray will be there." That was four days ago. I wonder if he'll still be there? Only one way to find out.

Creed rode up Nevada Street to the Gulch Road and followed it for the mile to Nevadaville and Pedro's Cantina, the last but not the least of the thirteen saloons in the mining town. The little wooden structure sandwiched between two log buildings wasn't much to look at on the outside. Creed tied Nimbus to a bull ring nailed to the false front of the cantina, and he stepped into the open doorway to survey the interior before entering. Pedro's wasn't much inside either. Four bare walls of vertical slabwood boards, a Franklin stove in one corner, a bar that consisted of two sturdy planks placed across three flour barrels, two square tables handmade from local lumber, each with four matching chairs, a backbar that was only a plank shelf for whiskey bottles and drinking glasses, and a dirt floor. The clientele were atypical of the town's saloons. Two dozen Mexicans, a few former slaves, and one Ute chief wrapped in an elk robe asleep in the corner opposite the stove.

"¿Eh, hombre? What do you want in here?" demanded the bartender, a portly Mexican with Aztec features, slicked-down

189

hair, and a bushy black mustache that was curled on the ends with wax.

Feeling every eye in the place shift toward him, Creed smiled and said, *"Quiero encountrar mi compadre aqui."*

"You have no friends here, *hombre*. Get out."

Creed wasn't in the mood to be hassled. He opened his coat and drew his Colt's. He leveled the revolver at the bartender, freezing every man in the joint. "I said, I want my friend here, and I don't feel like taking any horse shit from you or anybody else in this place. *¿Comprende, cabrón?"*

Ouray stirred from his slumber.

The bartender raised his hands and said, "Take him and get out."

"That's all I wanted to do in the first place," said Creed. "Ouray? Wake up, *amigo.*"

Ouray opened his eyes, surveyed the situation, and said, "You *Tejanos*. You make so much out of so little." He stood up. "Come, *mi amigo*. We will leave this place." He walked past the bar. "Pedro? *Adiós, mi amigo*. Ouray will come again when the whiskey is better here."

"My whiskey is as good as it will ever be," said Pedro.

"That is too bad," said Ouray, shaking his head. He stopped at the doorway, turned around, and added, "Ouray was hoping for better from you. *Adiós.*"

Creed backed out of the cantina. When he felt secure that nobody would follow them, he replaced the Colt's inside his waistband and turned to Ouray. "I need your help, *amigo.*"

"Yes, you do. How?"

"I need some horses."

"Horses?"

"Yes, three of them."

"You want Ouray to steal these horses?"

"No. I was hoping you might know where we could . . . uh . . . borrow some."

"Borrow horses?"

"Yes, borrow. I'll only need them for a short time. Tonight and tomorrow. Maybe until Monday."

"Monday?"

"The day after tomorrow."

Ouray nodded sagely. "You have found the man who can give back your name?"

"Yes, I have, but he's in the jail in Central City."

The Ute smiled and said, "Sheriff Billy Cozens has him, and you want to steal him away in the night. Yes?"

"Exactly," said Creed.

"Good. Ouray will get you the horses. You go back to the jail and wait behind it. Ouray will be along soon with the horses you need."

"Don't take too long," said Creed. "The sheriff is planning to move his prisoners to a safer place."

"What place is safer than the jail?"

"I don't know. I just know that he's gonna move them to some other place, and I want to get Quade away from him before he does."

Ouray nodded and said, "You go to the jail and wait. Go now. Ouray will come in time." He turned away and disappeared in the darkness.

Creed rode back to Central City and took a position on the hillside behind the jail. He waited.

The night air was crisp and invigorating. The stars sparkled like diamonds, and the moon shone in its fullness in the eastern sky. The tinny music of pianos, the laughter of drunken men, the shrill shrieks of lewd women giving false delight to their customers echoed down Nevada Gulch to Central City, which was strangely quiet. Too quiet. The lull before the storm? wondered Creed. Probably.

A trio of men carrying rifles hurried down Spring Street toward the jail. Creed recognized one of them as Charley

Utter. Damn! he thought. It looks like the sheriff has all his men in place now. He'll be moving those prisoners any minute. Damn! Where's that Indian and the horses?

No sooner did he have the thought than Ouray turned the corner from Nevada Street. He sat atop one horse, and he led another. Both animals were saddled. Damn! He didn't get enough horses. I told him to get three, not just two.

Utter and the two men with him entered the jail, apparently without seeing Ouray and the horses.

Ouray turned south on Spring Street as if he were headed for Russell Gulch. A subterfuge in case Utter and the others had seen him. As soon as he was certain that they hadn't or that they had and thought him no threat, he turned back and found Creed behind the jail.

"How did you know where I was?" asked Creed.

"Your horse catches the moonlight very well," explained Ouray as soon as he'd dismounted.

"Damn! I never thought of that. I hope those three men who just went into the jail didn't see him up here."

"If they did, it is too late now to hide."

"Yeah, you're right. Say, *amigo,* didn't I tell you to get three horses?"

"Yes, you did, but you already have one horse. One and two makes three, does it not?"

"Yes, but I was planning on having you take Nimbus and one of the horses down the road a piece toward Denver and wait for me and Quade to come along on the other two. We change horses there and go on to Denver."

"Why would you wish to do that?"

"Just in case a posse is chasing us. We'd have fresh horses, and that would allow us to outdistance them without too much trouble."

"No need for that, Creed."

"No?"

"No," said Ouray grimly.

"Do you know something that I don't know?"

"Yes."

Creed waited for Ouray to continue with his answer, but when the Ute failed to explain, the Texan said, "Well, what is it?"

"What is what, *mi amigo?*"

"What is it that you know that I don't know?"

"You do not need to know. Not now."

The back door to the jailhouse opened noisily, effectively forcing Creed to be silent. He stared at the lighted doorway.

Sheriff Cozens stood silhouetted against the light from within the jail. "All right," he said, "bring them out." He stepped into the night, followed by his five prisoners and three deputies, including Charley Utter. Cozens turned to his left at the bottom of the short stairs, taking a path that ran behind the buildings that faced Spring Street and emptied on Gregory Street, which was also the road to Black Hawk.

"Come," said Ouray. "We will follow them at a safe distance."

Creed stared at the Indian, wondering who was in charge of this raid.

Ouray ignored the Texan. He led the two borrowed horses down the hillside to the same path that Cozens had chosen to use.

Creed shrugged to himself and followed with Nimbus.

Cozens and his party left the path at Gregory Street, which paralleled Gregory Gulch, and they headed toward Black Hawk, walking at a brisk pace. The sheriff remained in the lead with the prisoners behind him and the three deputies, each carrying a rifle, bringing up the rear.

A simple plan of action developed in Ouray's head. He stopped at Gregory Street and waited for Creed to come to him, thus allowing the sheriff and his party to get farther ahead of them.

"Why did you stop?" whispered Creed.

"Wait," said Ouray. He allowed another minute to pass before answering Creed. "We must take this man from the sheriff before they reach Black Hawk. Ouray has decided how to do this."

"Ouray has decided? Don't I get a say in this?"

"No. Ouray is chief. Creed is brave warrior. We will do as Ouray says."

"All right, I suppose I can go along with that for now. What's your plan, *jefe?*"

Ouray outlined his scheme in simple terms. Creed was to ride across Gregory Gulch to Lawrence Street, follow it toward Black Hawk to the next bridge over the gulch, and cross back to Gregory Street. Ahead was Belden's Store at Gregory Point, the site of John Gregory's discovery in '59. Creed was to take up a position there and wait.

"What then?" asked the Texan.

"When the sheriff comes close to you, Ouray will ride up behind them. When they turn to see Ouray, you will come out of hiding and make them your prisoners. Does Creed understand Ouray?"

Creed leapt into the saddle. "I understand perfectly. I'll see you in a few minutes." He rode off toward Central City, crossed the Spring Street Bridge to Lawrence, and followed the road toward Black Hawk at a trot. He couldn't see Cozens and his party on the other side of the gulch when he passed them, but he could hear chains rattling and the men talking— one of the deputies mentioning that a rider was coming, and Utter telling him that the rider was on the other side of the gulch and that it shouldn't concern them. Another quarter of a mile along Lawrence, Creed saw the glow of light in the upstairs windows of Belden's Store, and shortly afterwards, he came to the second bridge across the gulch. He slowed Nimbus to a walk, crossed as quietly as possible back to Gregory Street, and rode back to the store where he took up a lookout post at the side of the building. He drew his Colt's and waited, but not for very long.

Cozens and his party came close to Belden's, and just as they were about to walk past the store, Ouray rode up behind them at a trot. Cozens turned around and halted the prisoners and the deputies.

Facing the unseen rider, Utter cocked his rifle and demanded, "Who goes there?"

Ouray reined in his mount and walked the animal toward the lawmen and criminals. "Charley Utter, is that you?" asked the Ute.

"I'll be damned," said Utter, recognizing the voice of an old friend in the darkness. He laughed and added, "It's only a drunken redskin." He relaxed, as did the others.

Creed took his cue. He crept from hiding, sneaking up behind Cozens and putting the muzzle of his revolver up to the nape of the sheriff's neck. He cocked the weapon and said, "Easy does it, Sheriff."

Cozens stiffened.

Utter, the other two deputies, and the five prisoners spun around as if they were so many soldiers responding to a drill sergeant's command.

"Don't anybody do anything stupid," said Creed. "I only want Quade. Just let me have him, and nobody gets hurt."

"Creed, is that you?" asked Utter.

"Who do you think it is, Charley?" growled Cozens. "Of course, it's him."

"Right as rain, Sheriff," said Creed. "Now you just let me have Quade, and we'll be out of your hair as quick as a cat can wink an eye."

"What are you gonna do with him?" asked Cozens.

"I'm not gonna kill him, if that's what you're worried about. I need him alive so he can tell the Army the truth for me."

"Good," said Cozens. "Take him and get the hell out of my county as fast as you can—and don't come back. If you do, I'll hunt you down and put you behind bars for a long, long time." He unlocked the chains around Quade's wrists. "The same goes for you, Quade. Don't come back here again. If you do, I won't be as likely to stop a lynch mob the next time one comes after you."

Ouray brought up the extra horse. He held tight to the reins, refusing to relinquish them to Quade, who didn't wait to be told to mount up.

"What about us?" asked the outlaw Jenkins. "Ain't you gonna set us free, too?"

"No," said Creed. "You'll have to get a jury to set you free, and frankly, I don't think you'll find twelve men stupid enough to do that. Leastways, not in these parts. Not after what you did around here." He backed away a step. "We'll be going now, Sheriff. Ouray, you and Quade get going. I'll be along in a minute."

The Ute obeyed, leading Quade's mount down the road toward Black Hawk.

As soon as they had vanished in the darkness, Creed said, "I wish we were parting on better terms, Sheriff."

"I wish you luck, Mr. Creed," said Cozens.

"Same here," said Utter.

"Thank you, Sheriff, Mr. Utter. *Adiós,* gents."

Creed disappeared around the corner of the store, untied Nimbus, mounted up, and dashed off after Ouray and Quade. He caught up with them in a minute. "All right, Quade," he said, "let's get something straight right off. We're riding down to Denver tonight, and tomorrow we're gonna get your wife and my brother's widow and my nephew, and we're all going back to Texas. You can ride sitting up, or I can strap you over the saddle. The choice is yours. If you try to run off, I'll shoot you in one leg, and if that doesn't work, I'll shoot you in the other leg. But no matter what, you're going back to Texas with me. Is that understood?"

"I understand, Slater, but you don't have to worry none about me. You just saved my life, and I ain't gonna forget that. I'll go back to Texas with you, and I'll gladly set the Army straight on that business in Mississippi."

"That's all I ask, Quade."

21

Dawn found Creed, Quade, and Ouray passing through the foothills near Golden. They had ridden all night to make certain that they weren't being followed by Sheriff Cozens or a lynch mob. They weren't.

"Well, it looks like we're in the clear now," said Quade cockily. "I'm sure beholden to you, Slater. You saved my life."

"That's the eighteenth time you've said that since we took you away from the sheriff," remarked Creed.

"I know, but I just want you to know how grateful I am to you for saving my life."

"That makes nineteen, and like I said the first time you said it, just tell the Army the truth about that raid in Mississippi and we'll call it even."

"You bet, Slater. As soon as we get to Texas."

"Fine," said Creed. He looked past Quade to Ouray, and the thought struck him that the Indian was still with them. Why? he wondered. Maybe I should ask him. "What about you, *jefe?* What will you do now?"

"Ouray will go to Denver with Creed."

"But why, *amigo?* I mean what's in Denver for you?"

"You."

Creed shook his head. "I don't understand it, but I guess it won't hurt anything for you to come along for the ride."

The trio rode on through the morning, arriving at the ferry across the South Platte just before noon. They had to wait for the ferryman to finish his dinner before he'd take them over to Denver.

In the city once again, Creed gave some thought to the immediate future. The Chicago Saloon was on the way to the Pacific House where Quade's wife resided. They would stop at the Chicago, and he would tell Hannah that he was back in town and that she should get her things together because he'd be calling for her and Little Dent first thing Monday morning. From there, they would ride across town to the Pacific House and tell Quade's wife that they were all leaving for Texas on the morrow.

After that, Creed would get a hotel room, and Ouray would— What about Ouray? What to do with him? He peered at the Indian again. Something spooky about that *hombre*. Yep, something spooky.

They came to the Chicago, and Creed turned Nimbus to the hitching rail out front of the saloon. "I'll only be a minute," he told Ouray and Quade just before dismounting and hitching Nimbus to the rail.

"I could use a drink myself," said Quade. "How about you, chief? Thirsty?"

"We should not go in there," said Ouray.

"Well, maybe you shouldn't," said Quade, "but I'm gonna wet my whistle while Slater talks to that woman he told us about. Stay out here in the hot sun if you like, but I'm going inside." He dismounted and followed Creed into the saloon.

Even on Sunday afternoons, the saloons in Denver did a thriving trade, but on this sabbath, Fourth Street and the vicinity was as quiet as a graveyard at midnight. The same was true of the Chicago when Creed and Quade entered it. A few men were standing at the far end of the bar having a casual drink, but they were the joint's only patrons.

Creed and Quade headed to the bar where Creed was surprised to find that Bob Stockton was the bartender.

"Afternoon, Mr. Stockton," said Creed in a friendly manner. "Kind of quiet around here. Someone die?"

"No," said Stockton. "Baseball game in town today. Just about every man, woman, and child is out to the park to watch the local nine play a club from Kansas City. Lot of money being bet today."

"Baseball, you say?" queried Creed. "I saw some Union soldiers playing the game during the war. I saw a game in New Orleans, too. Looked like fun. I've never played it myself, but I'd like to try it some day before I get too old to play games."

"Me, too," said Stockton impatiently. "So what are you doing here? Did you come to see Juanita again?"

"Yes, I did. Is she upstairs?"

"In her room. You can go up whenever you want."

Creed's eyes adjusted fully to the dim light of the saloon now, and for the first time, he noticed that one of the customers at the far end of the bar was Jimmy Stockton, his right arm in a sling. Damn! he thought. That troublemaker had to be here, didn't he? Well, I'll just ignore him, and maybe everything will be all right.

"Draw a beer for my friend, will you, Mr. Stockton?" said Creed. He dug a silver dollar from his coin pocket and laid it on the counter. He patted Quade on the shoulder and said, "Don't have too many, Marsh. It wouldn't do for you to be drunk when we take you home."

"I know my limit, Clete."

Creed smiled and said, "Good. Drink up, and I'll be back in a few minutes." He went upstairs to Hannah's room, knocked on the door, and called out, "Juanita, it's me. Slate Creed."

The door opened. Hannah stood to one side. "Come in,"

she said softly. After Creed was in the room, she closed the door behind him. "I didn't expect to see you again, Clete. Or at least not so soon as this."

"Well, things happened faster than I figured they would." He removed his hat, sat down on the bed, and told her about his experience in Central City the night before.

Down in the bar, Quade drained his first mug of beer and ordered another. Ouray slipped into the saloon quietly and sat down in a dark corner near the door and foot of the staircase. Jimmy Stockton left his drinking pal and drifted down the bar to Quade.

"Afternoon," said Quade cordially.

"Afternoon," said Jimmy. "I see that you're with that Reb, Creed. He a friend of yours?"

"That's right, he is," said Quade, not so friendly-like now. "What of it?"

Bob Stockton brought Quade his second beer. "Leave it alone, Jimmy," he said.

"I ain't doing nothing here, Bob. Just talking to Creed's friend. There ain't no harm in that now, is there?"

"I don't want you starting anything today, Jimmy."

"I ain't doing nothing, Bob."

"Well, just see that you don't."

"We're just talking. That's all."

Bob glared at his brother as he moved away behind the bar to busy himself elsewhere.

"Now where were we?" Jimmy asked Quade.

"You were asking me about my friend," said Quade.

"Yes, I was, wasn't I?"

"Well, what about him?"

"Known him long?"

"Since the start of the war. We joined up at the same time back home."

"Oh, so you're a Reb, too."

"What of it?"

"Oh, nothing," said Jimmy. "Nothing at all. The war's over, ain't it?"

"It is for some," said Quade.

"That's right, my friend. For some, but not for your friend Creed. You see, he had this nigger with him the last time I saw him, and Creed and his nigger jumped me, and the nigger grabbed me from behind and broke my shoulder."

"I see," said Quade. "So now you want revenge on my friend for what this nigger did to you, is that it?"

"Oh, no, not at all. Besides, how could I call him out when I got this broken shoulder? I'd be a damn fool to try anything while I'm in this condition, now wouldn't I?"

"That you would," said Quade.

"What was your name again?" asked Jimmy.

"I didn't say, but it's Marsh Quade."

"Glad to meet you, Marsh. Let me buy you a drink?"

Quade was amenable to that.

Upstairs, Creed finished telling Hannah about the night before in Central City. "So now we're back, and tomorrow we'll be leaving for Texas."

"How are we gonna git to Texas, Clete?" asked Hannah, sitting beside him.

"When the bank opens in the morning, I'm gonna draw out my money and buy us a couple of wagons and provisions for the journey home. As soon as we get loaded up, we're heading out. I'm not wasting any more time here than I have to. All you have to do is be ready to leave when the time comes."

"It ain't all that easy, Clete."

"Why isn't it?"

"Mr. Morton ain't gonna let me go."

"He can't stop you from going, Hannah."

"Yes, he can. I owe him money."

"You owe him money? How much?"

"I don't know for sure how much, but it's over a hundred dollars."

"How do you come to owe him so much money?"

"I don't rightly know, but he says it's for rent, food, and clothes for me and Little Dent."

Creed frowned and said, "Oh, I understand now. All right, I'll pay Morton for you."

"You got that kind of money, Clete?"

"Yes, I do."

"But how am I gonna pay you back, if you pay Mr. Morton for me?"

Creed stood up to leave. "You don't have to pay me back, Hannah. Just be my sister and be a good mother to my nephew. That's all the payment I'll ever need."

"Oh, Clete," she said, tears in her eyes. She jumped up, threw her arms around his neck, and kissed him.

Creed was too startled to do anything except let her have her way for a few seconds. When she didn't seem willing to end the embrace, he ended it for her. "You just be ready to leave tomorrow," he said.

With tears streaking her cheeks, she said, "I will, Clete. I will." She kissed him again. "Thank you, Clete. Thank you for both of us."

"Just be ready to leave." He opened the door. "I'll be by here in the morning. I'll see you then."

"We'll be ready," said Hannah.

From the top of the stairs, Creed saw Ouray sitting in the corner near the door. They exchanged nods as Creed descended the steps. Halfway down, Creed saw Quade at the bar drinking with Jimmy Stockton. Damn that little troublemaker, he thought. He didn't learn, did he? Well, maybe I can get Quade out of here without any trouble. He took the last step and stopped to speak with Ouray.

"It went well, *amigo?*" asked the Indian.

"Yes, it did, *jefe*. She'll be ready to leave tomorrow."

"*¡Muy bien!*" said Ouray. He nodded sideways. "Is that the *muchacho* who made trouble for Creed?"

Creed frowned and said, "That's him, all right."

"Be careful near him." The words should have been enough to warn Creed that danger lurked here, but to emphasize the caution, Ouray gave him a look that only another Indian could identify.

Seeing the sincerity in Ouray's eyes, Creed said softly, "I will." He moved toward the bar, taking the left flap of his coat in hand as he did. If young Stockton should make any sudden movements, he would be ready with his Colt's.

"Clete," said Quade as Creed stepped up to the bar beside him. "All done up there already?"

Creed eyed Jimmy, and for the first time, he noticed the sling on Stockton's right arm. "Yes, I'm all done upstairs," he said evenly.

"You really go for that Mexican bitch, don't you, Mr. Creed?" said Jimmy. He stood facing Creed.

"Listen up, Stockton," said Creed, squaring off to face Jimmy. "I'm only gonna say this once. If you want your other arm in a sling, just keep talking like that, and I'll gladly oblige you."

Bob came up to them. "I warned you to leave it alone, Jimmy," he said.

"Hey, I didn't mean nothing by that," said Jimmy defensively. "I was just trying to make conversation is all."

"Well, make it elsewhere," said Bob.

Creed glanced down at the pile of coins on the bar in front of Quade: eighty-five cents. He figured Quade had downed three beers, and that was enough. "Come on, Marsh. We'd best be leaving."

"What's your hurry?" asked Jimmy. "You haven't finished

the beer I bought for you, Marsh, and I'd like to buy you one, Mr. Creed, just as a way of saying that I ain't got no hard feelings about this." He patted his injured shoulder. "Set him up, Bob."

"Something tells me that you're not exactly sincere about that, Stockton."

Jimmy turned his back to the bar, leaned against it, and said, "Now that ain't so, Mr. Creed. I'm quite sincere about it. Hell, your nigger only broke my shoulder. He didn't kill me. Neither did you, for that matter. I'm grateful, Mr. Creed, and I want to show you how grateful I am. Let me buy you a beer." He smiled. "All right?"

"Let him buy you a beer, Clete," said Quade. "What's it gonna hurt?"

Creed let his guard down for a second. "All right," he said, "one beer." He turned to face the bar.

Bob went to draw the beer.

Jimmy slipped his left hand inside the sling, drew out a two-shot derringer, and started to point it at Creed's back.

"Creed!" shouted Ouray.

Creed twisted to face Jimmy.

So did Quade.

"Out of my way, asshole!" shouted Jimmy as he tried to push Quade aside for a clear shot at Creed.

Quade stumbled against Creed, preventing him from drawing his Colt's cleanly. To right himself, he grabbed Jimmy's gun hand, inadvertently bringing the muzzle of the pistol against his ribcage.

BANG!

Quade was jolted backwards. Creed caught him with his left arm and kept him from falling.

Jimmy freed himself from Quade's grip and backed away for a second try at Creed.

Bob grabbed the bungstarter from behind the backbar and

slammed it into the back of his brother's head.

Jimmy fell forward on his face, his head at Quade's feet. He was unconscious.

Quade felt a burning in his side. He opened his coat and saw his own blood staining his boiled shirt. He looked over his shoulder and said, "Sweet Jesus, Clete! I'm shot." His knees buckled.

Creed wrapped his other arm around Quade, lowered him slowly to the floor to a sitting position, and propped him against the bar.

Knife in hand, Ouray left his corner to come to them.

Bob dropped the bungstarter, grabbed his shotgun, cocked it, aimed it at Ouray, and said, "Hold it right there, Injun!"

Wisely, Ouray halted. He dropped the knife on the floor beside him. "Ouray goes to help his friend, not to harm your brother."

"All right, but leave the knife on the floor."

"Easy, Marsh," said Creed. He assessed the wound. Damn! he thought. The little sonofabitch shot him in the chest. "We need a doctor real quick." He pressed Quade's coat against the bleeding hole. "Hold that there, Marsh."

Ouray knelt beside them.

"Ermerins," gasped Quade.

"Ermerins?" queried Creed.

"Mrs. Ermerins," said Quade. "Her husband is a doctor. He's got an office over her store. Take me there and get Sal."

"He should not be moved," said Ouray. "His wound is too bad."

"I know that," said Creed. "Marsh, I'll fetch the doctor back here."

"And Sal, too?"

"And Sal, too," said Creed. He stood up, saw Stockton holding the shotgun on them, and, looking him straight in the eye, said, "If my friend dies, Mr. Stockton, so does your brother."

"And so will you," said Stockton.

"Maybe. Maybe not. Maybe you'll be joining them instead of me."

Stockton flinched.

Creed didn't. Without another word, he left the Chicago, jumped on Nimbus, and rode across town to find Dr. and Mrs. Ermerins enjoying their Sunday dinner in their apartment above the millinery store. "I'm sorry to interrupt your meal, Mrs. Ermerins," he said at the door, "but I need your husband to come with me to the Chicago Saloon right away. Mrs. Quade's husband has been shot."

"Shot? Oh, my!" she gasped, putting a hand over her mouth. She turned around to her husband, who watched them from the dining table. "Jacob, Mr. Creed says Mr. Quade has been shot at a saloon."

"Shot?" repeated the physician. He slid away from the table and stood up.

Creed moved past Mrs. Ermerins into the room. "I'm sorry to interrupt your meal, Doctor, but you've got to come quick. Marsh has been shot in the chest, and he's bleeding real bad. I'm afraid he might not make it if you don't hurry."

"Yes, of course. I'll get my bag." He disappeared into another room.

"Mrs. Ermerins, Marsh wanted me to fetch his wife for him, but I don't think there's enough time for me to do that right now."

"Of course. You go with Dr. Ermerins, and I'll fetch Sal for him. Where is this saloon where he was shot?"

"It's the Chicago. I'm not sure which street it is, but I do know that it's across the creek."

Dr. Ermerins returned with his medical bag.

"I'll find it," said Mrs. Ermerins. "You go on now."

Creed had the doctor ride double with him back to the Chicago, which had several more people in it now, including Dan Cooley, the policeman, who had charge of Jimmy Stockton in the back of the hall.

Bob Stockton and Ouray had picked up Quade and put him on the bar. Hannah had come downstairs with the other ladies in residence, and they had removed Quade's coat and shirt and had washed the blood from his skin while stopping the bleeding with a heavy compress. Quade was awake and lucid.

Ermerins removed the bandage and examined the wound. He replaced the dressing gingerly. The sadness in his eyes said everything.

Quade saw the look and knew that he had only a short time to live. "Clete," he gasped, "where's Sal?"

"She's coming, Marsh," said Creed. "Mrs. Ermerins is fetching her for you."

"Good. Good. I want to see her one more time before I die."

"You're not dying, Marsh," said Creed.

"This ain't the time for lying, Clete. This is the time for telling the truth, and that's what I want to do. I want to tell everybody that you didn't have nothing to do with that raid in Mississippi last year. Did you hear that Dr. Ermerins? I said that Clete Slater didn't have nothing to do with that raid in Mississippi last year."

"I heard you, Mr. Quade," said Ermerins, "but I don't understand what you're talking about."

"That's all right," said Quade. "Clete knows. He'll explain it to you later. Right now, it's enough that you know that he didn't have nothing to do with that raid." He scanned the room. "Get everybody close to hear me say it, Clete. They can all tell the Army for you that you had nothing to do with that raid in Mississippi last year. Get them all around me so I can tell them."

"Is he making some sort of confession, Mr. Creed?" asked the doctor.

"Yes, he is."

"Then you should have it written down."

"Yes, you're right," said Creed. He looked to Stockton and said, "I need a pencil and some paper, Mr. Stockton. Right now."

"Sure, I'll get some from the back room," said Stockton. He disappeared in that direction.

"Hold on, Marsh," said Creed. "We're gonna write down what you say, and then you can put your name on it, and everybody here can be witnesses to it."

"Good. That's good, Clete."

Stockton brought the pencil and paper, and Ermerins took down Quade's confession in which he exonerated Creed and named Jack Blackburn, Jasper Johnson, Dick Barth, Dick Spencer, Jonas Burr, and himself as the only men who raided a military supply train in Mississippi the previous year. He signed his name shakily but legibly, and everybody there who could write his own name signed the document as witnesses.

As Creed folded the confession and put it in an inside coat pocket, Sal Quade and Mrs. Ermerins entered the saloon. When she saw Quade on the bar, Sal burst into tears and threw herself over him.

"It's all right, Sal," said Quade as he patted her head, "I'm dying with a clear conscience. I told the truth about Clete and that business down in Mississippi last year. I won't be dying with that on my conscience."

"No, you can't die, Marsh. You can't, you can't. I love you, Marsh. You can't die like this. You can't."

"I love you, too, Sal." He coughed once. Blood trickled from the corners of his mouth. His eyes rolled up, and his lungs heaved a death sigh.

"No, no, no, no!" bawled Sal.

Creed turned to Stockton and said, "I told you what might happen if he died, didn't I?"

Stockton picked up the shotgun again and said, "And I told you what might happen, too."

"Your brother has to pay for this, Stockton."

"He will. He'll have a trial, and a judge and jury will decide how he'll pay for this man's life. They'll decide, Creed. Not you." Over his shoulder, he said, "Cooley, you'd better get Jimmy out of here."

Sal stopped her sobbing as Mrs. Ermerins tried to comfort her.

Creed looked from Stockton to Cooley as he brought Jimmy from the back of the room. Looking at Stockton again, he said, "All right. We'll let the law handle this."

"The law?" shrieked Sal. "I'll show you some law." She reached for Stockton's shotgun.

Stockton wrenched it away from her. It fired. BOOM!

Jimmy lurched backward, his chest filled with buckshot.

Creed pushed Sal aside and jumped Stockton, knocking him to the floor and wresting the shotgun from him. He got to his feet, holding the weapon on Stockton.

The bartender stood up slowly and glared at Creed.

"Never mind the law," said Creed softly. "Justice has already been served here."

"What?" mumbled Stockton, staring at Creed who was looking past him at Jimmy. Stockton turned slowly and saw his brother lying dead on the floor. "Oh, God, no!" He went to Jimmy, took him in his arms, and cried like a child.

Creed remembered his own brother, and with tears in his eyes, he broke the shotgun over the bar.

Epilogue

A cold wind swept down from the Rockies and brought a chill to the Plains.

Creed pulled the collar of his coat tighter around his neck to keep out the draft. His thoughts turned to his last three days in Denver.

Quade's death changed Creed's plans, although only slightly. He withdrew the balance of his funds from the First National Bank of Denver, as he'd intended to do, and he bought a covered wagon and a team of four mules to pull it. He paid off Hannah's so-called debt to Billy Morton, and he put her and Little Dent up at the Pacific House where he had chosen to stay this last time in the city. Instead of leaving on Monday, however, he decided to remain in Denver to see that Marshall Quade received a decent burial.

Much to Creed's surprise and comfort, Ouray also stayed in Denver. When Creed asked him why, the Ute replied that he only wanted to share some more time with him. Creed suspected a deeper reason, but he didn't push for it.

Creed paid for Quade's funeral, everything from the coffin to the minister. Only a few people attended the service: Creed, Sal, Ouray, Dr. and Mrs. Ermerins, and oddly, Clara Williams. After the funeral, she approached Sal and expressed her sympathy for her loss, saying, "I came to offer you an invitation to visit me at my home whenever you please, Mrs. Quade. I am also a widow, and I know what it's like to lose a husband."

"Thank you for the invitation, Mrs. Williams," said Sal, "but I won't be staying in Denver. I'm going back to Tennessee as soon as I can raise the fare."

"Tennessee? I thought I'd heard that you came here from Kentucky."

"Well, yes, we did, but I'm from Tennessee. My late husband was from Texas, and we went to Kentucky to visit relations of mine before coming here."

"I see. I also have relation in Kentucky. Logan County."

"Really? That's where my relations live."

"Excuse me, Mrs. Williams," said Creed, "but did you say Logan County?"

"Yes, I did, Mr. Creed. Don't tell me that you also have relations in Logan County."

"No, no relation there. I was posted in Logan County during the war for a few months, and I passed through there earlier this year when I was trying to find Mrs. Quade's husband."

"Is that right?"

"Yes, ma'am. In fact, Mrs. Quade's husband served in the same company with me."

"But that's not where I met Marsh," said Sal. "We met when his company was posted near my family's home at Wrencoe, Tennessee. After they left the area, I thought I'd never see Marsh again, but he came back after the war was over, and we were married."

"I have a cousin who had a romance like yours, Mrs. Quade," said Mrs. Williams, as she looked directly at Creed, "but her beau never came back for her."

"That's too bad," said Sal.

"Yes, it is," said Mrs. Williams, again looking at Creed. "She's had a broken heart ever since."

Feeling uncomfortable suddenly, Creed excused himself and went to speak to Ouray before he left for the mountains. "I just wanted to thank you one more time, *amigo*," he said. "Things didn't turn out exactly like I thought they would, but they never do, do they?"

"Sometimes they turn out better," said Ouray.

"Yeah, I suppose they do." Then something the Ute had said to him the night they took Quade from Sheriff Cozens came back to him. "Wait a minute. Back in Central City, you said that you knew something I didn't know. Are you gonna tell me that you saw all this happen in your vision?"

"No, not all. In the vision, Ouray saw two white men lying dead. Ouray thought one was Creed."

"And that's why you came with me to Denver? To save my life?"

Ouray shrugged. "Ouray was wrong. It happens."

They said good-bye and went their separate ways. Ouray back to his beloved mountains, and Creed with Hannah and Little Dent in the bed of the wagon and Marsh Quade's signed confession in his coat pocket back to the Chickasaw Nation.